Effective Technical Communication

科技英文

By Ted Knoy
柯泰德

Illustrated by Chen-Yin Wang
插圖：王貞穎

Ted Knoy is also the author of the following books in the Chinese Technical Writers' Series（科技英文寫作系列叢書）*and the Chinese Professional Writers' Series*（應用英文寫作系列叢書）：

An English Style Approach for Chinese Technical Writers
《精通科技論文寫作》

English Oral Presentations for Chinese Technical Writers
《做好英文會議簡報》

A Correspondence Manual for Chinese Writers 《英文信函參考手冊》

An Editing Workbook for Chinese Technical Writers
《科技英文編修訓練手冊》

Advanced Copyediting Practice for Chinese Technical Writers
《科技英文編修訓練手冊進階篇》

Writing Effective Study Plans 《有效撰寫讀書計畫》

Writing Effective Work Proposals 《有效撰寫英文工作提案》

Writing Effective Employment Application Statements
《有效撰寫求職英文自傳》

Writing Effective Career Statements 《有效撰寫英文職涯經歷》

Effectively Communicating Online 《有效撰寫英文電子郵件》

Writing Effective Marketing Promotional Materials 《有效撰寫行銷英文》

Effective Management Communication 《管理英文手冊》

Effective Business Communication 《商用英文》

This book is dedicated to my wife, Hwang Li Wen.

Table of Contents

· Describe the project background in which the managerial problem and project needs are introduced, with an emphasis on your group's role within the organization
調查性報告告知讀者特定管理問題的背景及合乎邏輯的需求回應，您的機構跟這個主題的相關程度多大？

· Discuss in detail the technical problem
目前的管理界情勢：管理問題後的工業背景？

· Cite examples of the problem that the company must solve to achieve its objective(s)
您的機構要解決什麼樣的問題？

· Emphasize to what extent that the problem affects the company's direction
這個問題影響到您機構的程度有多深？

· Highlight how failing to solve the problem would impact not only the company but also a particular field
這個沒有解決的問題會如何影響到您的機構及管理業界其他人？

· Summarize briefly how to solve the technical problem
要如何進行來解決這個管理問題？

· Describe how the project results contribute to a professional or academic field
管理方案對特定部門或領域的全面貢獻

· Apply for a specific job by referring to an advertisement, mutual friend or other source of information about a particular line of work
經由廣告、朋友及其他相關訊息得知的工作申請

· Summarize ones' academic and professional qualifications in relation to the needs of your potential employer
對未來工作的個人學術及相關專業特質總結

· Compliment the organization that you are applying to and state how work there would benefit one's career goals
讚揚要申請工作的機構及說明其對個人工作目標所產生的利益

· Sum up the memo with one main theme or selling point
總結主要論點

· Invite the reader to contact you for an interview
邀請讀者給予面試機會

· Request professional training
科技訓練申請

Table of Contents

Foreword

Professional writing is essential to the international recognition of Taiwan's commercial and technological achievements. The Chinese Professional Writers' Series seeks to provide a sound English writing curriculum and, on a more practical level, to provide Chinese speaking professionals with valuable reference guides. The series supports professional writers in the following areas:

Writing style

The books seek to transform old ways of writing into a more active and direct writing style that better conveys an author's main ideas.

Structure

The series addresses the organization and content of reports and other common forms of writing.

Quality

Inevitably, writers prepare reports to meet the expectations of editors and referees/reviewers, as well as to satisfy the requirements of journals. The books in this series are prepared with these specific needs in mind.

Effective Technical Communication is the ninth book in The Chinese Professional Writers' Series.

前　言

　　Effective Technical Communication（科技英文）爲「應用英文寫作系列」（The Chinese Professional Writers' Series）之第九本書，書中練習題部分主要是幫助國人糾正常犯寫作錯誤，由反覆練習中，進而熟能生巧提升有關英文商業策略的寫作能力。

　　「應用英文寫作系列」將針對以下內容，逐步協助國人解決在英文寫作上所遭遇之各項問題：

A. 寫作型式：把往昔通常習於抄襲的寫作方法轉換成更積極主動的寫作方式，俾使讀者所欲表達的主題意念更加清楚，更進一步糾正國人寫作口語習慣。

B. 方法型式：指出國內寫作者從事英文寫作或英文翻譯時常遇到的文法問題。

C. 內容結構：將寫作的內容以下面的方式結構化：目標、一般動機、個人動機。並了解不同的目的和動機可以影響報告的結構，由此，獲得最適當的報告內容。

D. 內容品質：以編輯、審查委員的要求來寫作此一系列之書籍，以滿足讀者的英文要求。

Introduction

This handbook orients technical professionals on the essentials of proficient communication in the workplace. How to write a problem analysis report is described first, including the project background in which the managerial problem and project needs are highlighted, a detailed discussion of the technical problem, examples of the problem that the company must solve to achieve its objective(s), an emphasis on the extent to which the problem affects the company's direction, the consequences of failing to solve the problem for both the company and a particular field, as well as a brief summary on how to solve the technical problem. How to write a recommendation report is then detailed, including the objectives, methodology and anticipated results to solve the technical problem, the nature of the problem, suggestions on how to solve the problem, a strategy outline for achieving the project goal, an emphasis on how the company would benefit from achieving the set goal(s), and a summary of how the larger industry or field would benefit from achieving the project goal(s). Next, how to write a persuasive report is introduced by citing a statistic or recent trend to attract the readers' interest in a particular topic, describing how reader's interests are addressed in the project planning and strategy, as well as customer service, discussing the feasibility of project success in terms of methodology, strategy and customer service, highlighting the anticipated benefits of project success, and summarizing the steps needed to ensure project success. Additionally, how to compile an informal technical report is discussed, including the managerial motivations in undertaking this project, the industrial setting in terms of customer concerns and the project group's priorities, the problem to be solved, the project goals, the project methodology, the main results of the project, and contribution to a professional or academic field. Finally, instructions are given on how to write effective correspondence for an employment application, training application and employment recommendation.

Each unit begins and ends with three visually represented situations that provide essential information to help students in various forms of technical communication. Additional oral practice, listening comprehension, reading comprehension and writing activities, relating to those three situations, help students to understand how the visual representation relates to the ultimate goal of writing effective technical communication. An Answer Key makes this book ideal for classroom use. For instance, to test a student's listening comprehension, a teacher can first read the text that describes the situations for a particular unit. Either individually or in small groups, students can work through the exercises to produce concise and well-structured technical communication.

簡 介

　　本書中的問題分析報告，告知讀者特定管理問題的背景、機構要解決什麼樣的問題，以及要如何來解決這個管理問題。調查性與建議性報告告知讀者管理目標、方法論及預期的結果，以求解決特定的管理問題，以及機構如何實行這個目標來達成可見的立即利益。其中也包括對管理界其他人造成的利益。非正式實用工程技術報告描述管理方案所關心的事項，闡明特定部門或客戶所關心的工業環境、管理方案方法論的細節描述、管理方案主要成果總結、管理方案對特定部門或領域的全面貢獻。章節說服力的展現部分，主要描述如何引起讀者注意，引導讀者預想計畫、策略或服務實行後的成果，最後採取特定行動達成目標。本書最後還包括求職申請信函、科技訓練申請信函，以及推薦信函的撰寫說明。

　　本書中的每個單元呈現三個視覺化的情境，經由以全民英語檢定為標準而設計的口說訓練、聽力、閱讀及寫作四種不同功能，來強化英文總體能力。此外，書後所附的解答使得本書也非常適合在課堂上使用，教師可以先描述單元情境，讓學生藉由書中的練習，循序在短期內完成。不論是小組或個人，皆可藉書中的練習，寫出更明白精確的科技英文報告及其相關文件。

Unit One

Problem Analysis Reports
問題分析報告

- Describe the project background in which the managerial problem and project needs are introduced, with an emphasis on your group's role within the organization
  調查性報告告知讀者特定管理問題的背景及合乎邏輯的需求回應，您的機構跟這個主題的相關程度多大？

- Discuss in detail the technical problem
  目前的管理界情勢：管理問題後的工業背景？

- Cite examples of the problem that the company must solve to achieve its objective(s)
  您的機構要解決什麼樣的問題？

- Emphasize to what extent that the problem affects the company's direction
  這個問題影響到您機構的程度有多深？

- Highlight how failing to solve the problem would impact not only the company but also a particular field
  這個沒有解決的問題會如何影響到您的機構及管理業界其他人？

- Summarize briefly how to solve the technical problem
  要如何進行來解決這個管理問題？

Vocabulary and related expressions

express concern over	對……事表示關切
intangible capital asset	無形資本資產
tangible assets	有形資產
intellectual capital	智慧財產權
heighten the importance of	提升……的重要性
skyrocketing to	猛然上升（物價）飆漲（失業率）攀升
underrating	低估
substandard lending practices	不合乎標準的放款作法
prospective customers	潛在客戶
creditworthiness	信譽可靠
varying degrees of risk	不同的風險程度
severity of this problem	這個問題的嚴重性
easily incurred debts	容易招致債務
budget deficits	預算赤字
turnover rate	周轉率
in the face of	面對；面臨；因應
pertinent	有關；恰當的；適合的
customer retention	保留客戶
most qualified vendor	最合格的供應商
severe budgetary constraints	嚴苛的預算限制
stringent mandates	嚴格的任務
potential environmental hazards	環境隱含潛在的危險
waste disposal firm	廢物回收處理公司
medical waste management	醫療用品廢棄管理
efficient distribution	高效率的經銷體系
substantial investment	大量的投資
incapacitated	無法勝任；失去維生能力
outsourcing agencies	國外採購代理人（公司）
widespread customer dissatisfaction	客戶普遍感到不滿意
an objective means of evaluating	客觀的評估方式（管理）

Situation 1

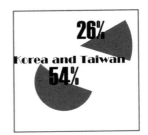

Situation 2

Situation 3

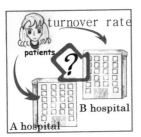

A Write down the key points of the situations on the preceding page, while the instructor reads aloud the script from the Answer Key. Alternatively, students can listen online at www.chineseowl.idv.tw.

Situation 1

_____

_____

_____

Situation 2

_____

_____

_____

Situation 3

_____

_____

_____

B Oral practice I

Based on the three situations in this unit, write three questions beginning with **Why**, and answer them. The questions do not need to come directly from these situations.

Examples

Why do financial institutions tend to underrate a company's value? They fail to consider intellectual capital assets.

Why will knowledge increasingly dominate efforts to create a competitive edge and generate wealth?

because it is the most fundamental intangible capital asset

1._____

_____

2._____

_____

3._____

_____

C Based on the three situations in this unit, write three questions beginning with **How**, and answer them. The questions do not need to come directly from these situations.

Examples

How is a higher risk of defaulting on loans incurred?

by substandard lending practices

How do banks encourage prospective customers to hold multiple credit cards?

by relaxing approval and credit reference procedures

1._____

_____

2._____

_____

3._____

_____

D Based on the three situations in this unit, write three questions beginning with **What**, and answer them. The questions do not need to come directly from these situations.

Examples

What does the hospital have difficulty in doing?

retaining current patients and reducing the turnover rate of patients who go to other medical centers for treatment

What factors have led to the implementation of a Global Budget System?

the extremely competitive medical market sector in Taiwan and budget deficits caused by the island's National Health Insurance scheme

1._____

_____

2._____

_____

3._____

_____

E Write questions that match the answers provided.

1._____

_____

the information age

2._____

_____

owing to the inability to identify either the degree of risk or the reasons to
further exacerbate credit card debt

3._____

_____

retaining current patients and reducing the turnover rate of those who are going
to other medical centers for treatment

F Listening Comprehension I

Situation 1

1. What will increasingly dominate efforts to create a competitive edge and generate wealth?

    A. a company's value

    B. knowledge

    C. tangible assets

2. Why do financial institutions tend to underrate a company's value?

    A. because they do not include tangible assets

    B. because their relative importance has declined

    C. because they fail to consider intellectual capital assets

3. What is a priority?

    A. measuring the value of tangible assets that can be quantified in a company

    B. determining exactly how an organization should assess its intellectual competency

    C. measuring the value of companies without incorporating intellectual capital

4. What evidence suggests the heightened importance of intellectual capital?

    A. the numerous companies that rely almost completely on intellectual assets for generating revenue

    B. the fact that online gaming ranks at the top of the gaming industry

    C. the fact that the global economy has moved into the information age

5. What prevents an understanding of how intellectual capital affects the on-line gaming market?

    A. the inability to measure the value of tangible assets that can be quantified in a company

    B. the inability to emphasize the ownership of tangible capital rather than intangible assets

C. the inability to measure the value of companies without incorporating intellectual capital

Situation 2

1. How do banks encourage prospective customers to hold multiple credit cards?

    A. by identifying both varying degrees of risk and reasons for credit card debt

    B. by explaining the increasing popularity of credit cards in Taiwan

    C. by relaxing approval and credit reference procedures

2. What has led to serious domestic competition?

    A. the inability to control effectively the spiraling of outstanding debts

    B. the increasing popularity of credit cards in Taiwan

    C. the fact that the average Taiwanese has an average of 2.8 cards

3. How many credit cards are available domestically?

    A. 6,500

    B. 6,321

    C. 4,500

4. What will further exacerbate the bank lending crisis in Taiwan?

    A. the inability to identify either the degree of risk or the reasons for credit card debt

    B. the inability to identify both varying degrees of risk and reasons for credit card debt

    C. the inability to incorporate the characteristics associated with the lifestyles of such customers

5. What have few studies measured?

    A. the characteristics associated with factors that contribute to easily incurred debts

    B. substandard lending practices

    C. varying degrees of risk among potential credit card customers

Situation 3

1. What has received increasing attention?

    A. a Global Budget System

    B. patient turnover rate

    C. new and return patients

2. What must hospitals concentrate their operational effort on?

    A. attracting new patients

    B. retaining current patients

    C. implementing a Global Budget System

3. What do hospitals prioritize?

    A. incorporating a novel set of management strategies that emphasize customer retention within the medical sector

    B. determining patient turnover rates precisely

    C. attracting new patients

4. What should a novel set of management strategies emphasize?

    A. budget deficits caused by the island's National Health Insurance scheme

    B. the turnover rate of customers in the medical sector

    C. customer retention within the medical sector

5. What do conventional approaches not differentiate between?

    A. retaining current patients and reducing the turnover rate of patients who go to other medical centers for treatment

    B. new and return patients

    C. the extremely competitive medical market sector in Taiwan and budget deficits caused by the island's National Health Insurance scheme

G Reading Comprehension I
Select the word or expression whose meaning is closest to the meaning of the underlined word or expression in the following passages.

Situation 1

1. For instance, on-line gaming companies <u>emphasize</u> the ownership of intangible capital rather than tangible assets.

   A. whitewash

   B. reiterate

   C. mute

2. Online gaming ranks at the top of the gaming industry, with generated revenues of US$1 billion in 1999, <u>skyrocketing</u> to US$2 billion in 2002.

   A. cascading

   B. escalating

   C. precipitating

3. According to the International Data Corporation (2003), in 2002, the on-line gaming market was 533,000,000 units in the Asian Pacific region, with South Korea and Taiwan <u>leading</u> the way, accounting for 54% and 26%, respectively.

   A. piloting

   B. superseding

   C. supplanting

4. The inability to measure the value of companies without <u>incorporating</u> intellectual capital not only leads to an underrating of their value, but also prevents an understanding of how intellectual capital affects the on-line gaming market.

   A. sidelining

   B. obviating

C. coalescing

5. Therefore, a novel index based on the analysis <u>hierarchy</u> process (AHP) must be developed to determine the value of the intellectual capital of on-line gaming companies.

A. decentralization

B. pecking order

C. nihilism

Situation 2

1. The severity of this problem is indicated by the fact that the average Taiwanese has an average of 2.8 cards from the currently available 6,321 credit cards available domestically, with credit card debt at 46% of the credit limit.

A. exuberance

B. starkness

C. fervor

2. The inability to identify either the degree of risk or the reasons for credit card debt will further <u>exacerbate</u> the bank lending crisis in Taiwan, ultimately threatening the survival of credit cooperatives owing to the inability to control effectively the spiraling of outstanding debts.

A. placate

B. appease

C. provoke

3. The inability to identify either the degree of risk or the reasons for credit card debt will further exacerbate the bank lending crisis in Taiwan, ultimately threatening the survival of credit cooperatives owing to the inability to control effectively the <u>spiraling</u> of outstanding debts.

A. convoluted

B. ardent

C. steadfast

4. Therefore, a novel evaluation method must be developed to identify credit card customers that incorporate the characteristics associated with the lifestyles of such customers and factors that <u>contribute</u> to easily incurred debts.

A. diminish

B. withhold

C. proffer

5. Therefore, a novel evaluation method must be developed to identify credit card customers that incorporate the characteristics associated with the lifestyles of such customers and factors that contribute to easily <u>incurred</u> debts.

A. induced

B. abstained

C. obviated

Situation 3

1. Incapable of determining patient turnover rates precisely, our hospital could face considerable expense in attracting new patients in the face of shrinking <u>subsidies</u> from the National Health Insurance scheme, ultimately lowering our competitiveness.

A. reparation

B. mulct

C. endowment

2. Incapable of determining patient turnover rates precisely, our hospital could face considerable expense in attracting new patients in the face of <u>shrinking</u> subsidies from the National Health Insurance scheme, ultimately lowering our competitiveness.

A. diminution

B. increment

C. augmentation

3. The inability to address effectively patient turnover rate makes the statistical approaches used to determine the samples in pertinent studies <u>inaccurate</u>.

A. specious

B. meticulous

C. judicious

4. Therefore, a novel prediction model must be developed to <u>identify</u> the turnover rate of customers in the medical sector.

A. obscure

B. becloud

C. peg

5. Administrators should incorporate a novel set of management strategies that emphasize customer <u>retention</u> within the medical sector.

A. extrication

B. uprooting

C. assimilation

H Common elements in writing a problem analysis report 問題分析報告 include the following elements:

a. 簡介：您的機構跟這個主題的相關程度多大？

範例 i

During our most recent board meeting, quality control engineers expressed concern over our company's low production yield of flip chip packages and low accuracy in predicting the fatigue life of such packages.

範例 ii

At a recent meeting, administrators discussed ways in which to enhance the global competitiveness ranking of Taiwan in the IMD World Competitiveness Scoreboard

b. 目前的管理界情勢：管理問題後的工業背景？

範例 i

As is well known, geometric parameters significantly affect the reliability of flip chip packaging under thermodynamic loading. Based on basic material mechanics, a higher solder joint height implies a larger shear force that the solder joint can bear. Moreover, several works have also concluded that cracks occur in a solder joint when a package is under critical thermodynamic loading. Furthermore, certain manufacturing issues, such as packaging falling-off problems, solder bridging and misalignment are also related to the design of the pad and solder joint.

範例 ii

Taiwan's global competitiveness ranking in the IMD World Competitiveness Scoreboard is falling. Taiwan ranked 16th in 1998, 18th in 1999, and 22nd in

2000, with its lowest performance, 23rd, in the last decade of 1997. Although many countries originally ranked behind Taiwan, for example, Austria, Belgium, France, Iceland, Japan, New Zealand, and Sweden, they have since surpassed the island. Moreover, mainland China ranked 11 slots behind Taiwan in 1999, and 9 behind Taiwan in 2000. The gap between Taiwan and mainland China is shrinking. The narrowest gap over the last decade was of four places in 1997.

c. 管理問題：您的機構要解決什麼樣的問題？

範例 i

However, geometric parameters of a C4 type solder joint still can not accurately predict the reliability of flip chip packaging under thermodynamic loading. Indeed, many engineers have tried to predict the geometric parameters of a C4 type solder joint using an energy-based method and analytical models. One of them simulated the C4 type solder joint as a semi-spherical high-lead bump buried into the eutectic solder; however the simulation lacks accuracy when the external loading increases. Besides, the above methodology ignores the effects of gravity. Moreover, the semi-spherical high-lead bump can not simulate the high-lead bump when the solder pad sizes vary.

範例 ii

A contributing factor to the fall in Taiwan's IMD World Competitiveness ranking is the IMD Competitiveness Simulations' neglecting interactions among factors. These simulations involve 20 strengths and 20 weaknesses of each nation. If nations plan to upgrade their global competitiveness ranking, they need merely to improve their 20 weaknesses. Although the IMD runs the simulation to help policy makers to focus on and prioritize the key competitiveness issues facing their countries, they neglect the criteria's correlation. For example, if Taiwan improves its standing in relation to a weak criterion, Growth In Direct Investment

Stocks Inward, its standing in relation to another strong criterion, Gross Domestic Savings Real Growth, will fall.

d. 問題的嚴重性：這個問題影響到您機構的程度有多深？

範例 i

For instance, an accuracy of less than 5% for the geometric parameters prevents engineers from either predicting the fatigue life or enhancing the yield of a flip chip package.

範例 ii

More specifically, using the IMD Competitiveness Simulations possibly causes policy makers to reach inaccurate decisions. To gain entry into the WTO, Taiwan has drawn up a re-engineering plan, including financial liberalization and strengthening of financial supervision, to develop Taiwan as a global logistics center and a regional operations center of the Asia-Pacific region. Such a plan also aims to develop high-tech industries with venture capital in 2001.

e. 問題的牽涉性：這個沒有解決的問題會如何影響到您的機構及管理業 界其他人？

範例 i

Under these circumstances, engineers can not predict the correct geometric parameters of a C4 type solder joint when the design factors vary. Therefore, engineers can neither predict the fatigue life nor enhance the yield of a flip chip package.

範例 ii

The inability to achieve an accuracy of 50% in the IMD Competitiveness Simulations makes it impossible to increase Taiwan's world competitiveness ranking.

f. 管理需求：要如何進行來解決這個管理問題？

範例 i

Therefore, an analytical geometry method must be developed, capable of accurately predicting the geometric parameters of practical C4 type solder joint in flip chip technology after a reflow process.

範例 ii

Therefore, a novel competitiveness model must be developed, capable of integrating a global optimization algorithm into the IMD World Competitiveness Model.

Problem Analysis Reports
問題分析報告

In the space below, write a problem analysis report.

_____

_____

_____

_____

_____

_____

_____

_____

_____

_____

_____

Look at the following examples of a problem analysis report.

範例 i

簡介 During our most recent board meeting, software engineers expressed concern over the many personnel hours involved in designing a rule base to represent the multi-state property. 目前的管理界情勢 Many machine learning and optimization application-related problems are solved by GA with the multi-state property. For instance, in chess, a good player often employs various strategies based on his opponent's moves, the game's progress, or the chess clock. Therefore, an intelligent chess playing program should consider the multi-state property to perform more effectively. Consider stock market investments as another example. Investors adopt various strategies according to whether the market is up or down. This behavior implies that a decision support system for investment should consider the multi-state property. Applying various strategies to distinct states of a problem is natural. A different solution or strategy should be employed by varying problem solving states to achieve the global optimum. 管理問題 However, conventional methods cannot solve multi-state problems. Although genetic algorithms are widely applied to machine learning and optimization, conventional GAs have not received much attention . Conventional approaches can use human designed rule bases to represent a multi-state solution, and employ GAs to alter the rule base. However, to our knowledge, no systematic method has been developed for dealing with the multi-state property in a GA-implemented system. 問題的嚴重性 If the solution varies with the problem state in a multi-state problem, conventional methods neglect the multi-state property and yield an inaccurate and unfeasible solution. For example, an investment decision support system that adopts a single strategy, regardless of whether the market is up or down, leads to an unsuccessful investment. 問題的牽涉性 Although a rule base can be used to represent the multi-state property, designing the rule base requires many manhours. 管理需求 Therefore, an effective GAs model must be developed, capable of deriving an optimal solution for each state in a multi-state problem.

範例 ii

簡介 Software engineers in our department recently expressed concern over difficulty in upgrading software and hardware in network management systems. 目前的管理界情勢 Intranets are extensively used by enterprises to accelerate commercial activities. Different operating systems and technologies are combined within the intranet infrastructures of enterprises. Therefore, maintaining a stable network environment is critical. A network management system may help enterprises to maintain efficiently a stable intranet efficiently. 管理問題 However, conventional network management systems are too expensive and complicated for implementation in an enterprise's intranet. 問題的牽涉性 Completely installing a network management system requires at least five engineers working full time for more than 6 months. Moreover, enterprises must spend another six months to train their employees and customize the system. Introducing a conventional network management system to an enterprise also requires additional machinery. Enterprises may need to modify the intranet infrastructure to fulfill the general requirements of a network management system. 問題的牽涉性 Additionally, enterprises may have difficulty in upgrading software and hardware since they must spend much to maintain the system, train operators, and install the server. 管理需求 Therefore, a novel web-based system in a PC-LAN environment must be developed, capable of detecting network problems. This system can provide an efficient and inexpensive solution for an enterprise to maintain a stable network environment.

Situation 4

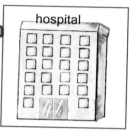

Situation 5

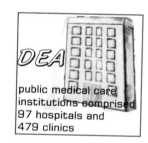

Situation 6

I Write down the key points of the situations on the preceding page, while the instructor reads aloud the script from the Answer Key. Alternatively, students can listen online at www.chineseowl.idv.tw.

Situation 4

_____

_____

_____

Situation 5

_____

_____

_____

Situation 6

_____

_____

_____

J Oral practice II
Based on the three situations in this unit, write three questions beginning with **Why**, and answer them. The questions do not need to come directly from these situations.

Examples

Why did hospital administrators recently express concern over how to select the most qualified vendor?

to handle medical waste produced by the hospital

Why do Taiwanese hospitals face tremendous pressure over medical waste produced?

They must effectively cope with not only the severe budgetary constraints of the national health insurance scheme, but also stringent mandates on medical waste treatment from the Environmental Protection Administration.

1._____

_____

2._____

_____

3._____

_____

K Based on the three situations in this unit, write three questions beginning with **What**, and answer them. The questions do not need to come directly from these situations.

Examples

What have rapid changes in Taiwan's healthcare environment led to?

a limitation of medical resources that make efficient distribution essential

What is a priority of health organizations?

efficient distribution

1._____

_____

2._____

_____

3._____

_____

L Based on the three situations in this unit, write three questions beginning with *How* and answer them. The questions do not need to come directly from these situations.

Examples

How can hospital administrators select the most productive outsourcing agencies?

by evaluating outsourced nursing care attendants

How does a rapidly growing elderly population pose a major challenge for long-term care management?

Immediate solutions are required, given changing family structures and the frequency of chronic illnesses.

1.＿＿＿＿＿＿＿＿＿＿＿＿＿＿＿＿＿＿＿＿＿＿＿＿＿

　＿＿＿＿＿＿＿＿＿＿＿＿＿＿＿＿＿＿＿＿＿＿＿＿＿

2.＿＿＿＿＿＿＿＿＿＿＿＿＿＿＿＿＿＿＿＿＿＿＿＿＿

　＿＿＿＿＿＿＿＿＿＿＿＿＿＿＿＿＿＿＿＿＿＿＿＿＿

3.＿＿＿＿＿＿＿＿＿＿＿＿＿＿＿＿＿＿＿＿＿＿＿＿＿

　＿＿＿＿＿＿＿＿＿＿＿＿＿＿＿＿＿＿＿＿＿＿＿＿＿

M Write questions that match the answers provided.

1._____

_____

nearly 300 metric tons of medical waste daily

2._____

_____

14,474

3._____

_____

a uniform management approach to ensure the quality of service

N Listening Comprehension II

Situation 4

1. How many hospital clinics operate in Taiwan?

   A. 120,000

   B. 17,500

   C. 300

2. Why is the environmental protection sector just beginning to address harmful waste emitted by the waste treatment sector?

   A. largely because of stringent mandates on medical waste treatment from the Environmental Protection Administration

   B. largely because of the lack of effective management experience in closely monitoring daily operations

   C. largely because of the limited scope of services that medical waste disposal firms provide

3. What do Taiwanese hospitals lack?

   A. stringent mandates on medical waste treatment from the Environmental Protection Administration

   B. subjective judgment and previous experience

   C. an objective criterion for selecting the most appropriate waste disposal firm and evaluating its performance

4. What creates potential environmental hazards and increases operating expenses?

   A. hospitals failing to comply with the severe budgetary constraints of the national health insurance scheme

   B. hospitals failing to adhere to stringent mandates on medical waste treatment from the Environmental Protection Administration

   C. hospitals disposing of large amounts of medical waste to ensure sanitation and personal hygiene

5. What percentage of daily medical waste daily is infectious?

    A. 12%

    B. 15%

    C. 20%

Situation 5

1. Why is efficient distribution essential?

    A. because efficient distribution is a priority of health organizations

    B. because rapid changes in Taiwan's healthcare environment lead to a limitation of medical resources

    C. because all hospitals utilize resources to provide many services

2. How many public and private medical institutions were operating in Taiwan as of the end of 1992?

    A. 13,170

    B. 14,174

    C. 14,474

3. What is an important measure of hospital performance?

    A. allocation of medical resources to hospitals by government

    B. the efficiency with which inputs are used to produce these services

    C. aggregative performance indicators such as return on investment (ROI), residual income (RI) and profitability

4. Why should state-level administrators analyze the productivity of each hospital?

    A. to enhance the performance of hospitals

    B. to provide many services, which are the output of healthcare organizations

    C. to determine whether resources are being utilized effectively

5. Why is the efficiency of public hospitals a priority?

    A. because of the substantial investment made by governments in healthcare

B. because of those factors that enhance the performance of hospitals

C. because of the management direction based on analytic methods that accurately reflect the efficiency of the healthcare services they provide

Situation 6

1. What requires immediate solutions?

   A. hospital-subsidized respiratory care centers

   B. long-term care management

   C. respiratory care wards

2. Why is it difficult to ensure quality of service among nursing care attendants?

   A. They are not always mentally and physically healthy.

   B. They are restricted in terms of age, education or experience.

   C. They lack a uniform management approach.

3. What has further contributed to the outsourcing of nursing care attendants?

   A. an emphasis on controlling personnel costs while maintaining high-quality services

   B. concern over how to evaluate outsourced nursing care attendants to select the most productive outsourcing agencies

   C. an objective means of evaluating the quality of nursing care attendants

4. What do relatives or patients that directly employ a nursing care attendant lack?

   A. basic healthcare training skills and knowledge of hospital or governmental infrastructure

   B. an adequate number of outsourcing agencies for nursing care attendants

   C. adequate evaluative criteria to select the most appropriate care provider

5. Why is a further decline in hospital revenues possible?

   A. widespread customer dissatisfaction and increasing management difficulty

   B. the inability to manage effectively the quality of service that nursing care attendants provide

   C. the lack of standardized training for nursing care attendants

O Reading Comprehension II
Select the word or expression whose meaning is closest to the meaning of the underlined word or expression in the following passages.

Situation 4

1. While the ability to handle medical waste efficiently depends on the ability of hospitals to adopt <u>sound</u> waste management practices and coordinate their efforts with waste disposal firms, Taiwanese hospitals lack an objective criterion for selecting the most appropriate waste disposal firm and evaluating its performance, but rely on their own subjective judgment and previous experience.

   A. solvent

   B. rinkydink

   C. gossamer

2. While the ability to handle medical waste efficiently depends on the ability of hospitals to adopt sound waste management practices and <u>coordinate</u> their efforts with waste disposal firms, Taiwanese hospitals lack an objective criterion for selecting the most appropriate waste disposal firm and evaluating its performance, but rely on their own subjective judgment and previous experience.

   A. disarray

   B. embroil

   C. synchronize

3. According to Department of Health statistics, approximately 17,500 hospital clinics, operating domestically with a bed capacity of roughly 120,000, produce nearly 300 metric tons of medical waste daily, of which 15% is <u>infectious</u>, which value is increasing.

A. innocuous

B. pestilent

C. aseptic

4. Given the growth in medical waste, the inability of hospitals to adopt an objective means of evaluating a waste disposal firm and its performance may lead to <u>inappropriate</u> selection and higher operational costs, necessitating the development of an effective means of objectively evaluating the performance of waste disposal firms, thus reducing overhead costs and improving medical waste management.

A. off base

B. congruous

C. germane

5. Since most hospitals contract waste disposal firms to handle their waste, administrators need a reliable method for contracting the most appropriate firm to monitor closely and reduce <u>expenditures</u> associated with this process.

A. kitty

B. capital investment

C. nest egg

Situation 5

1. All hospitals utilize resources to provide many services, which are the output of healthcare organizations. Thus, the efficiency with which inputs are used to produce these services is an important <u>measure</u> of performance.

A. yard stick

B. smoke screen

C. pretense

2. Of the 14,474 public and private medical institutions that were <u>operating</u> in Taiwan as of the end of 1992, public medical care institutions comprised 97

hospitals and 479 clinics while private institutions comprised 728 hospitals and 13,170 clinics.

A. abeyant

B. dormant

C. functioning

3. Given the <u>substantial</u> investment made by governments in healthcare, the efficiency of public hospitals is a priority.

A. momentous

B. ephemeral

C. tenuous

4. The inability to measure this efficiency almost prevents the <u>allocation</u> of medical resources to hospitals by government.

A. allotment

B. accretion

C. procurement

5. An analysis must be based not only on the <u>efficiency</u> of healthcare services offered by public hospitals, as determined using data envelopment analysis (DEA), but also on those factors that enhance the performance of hospitals such that administrators can revise directions in management accordingly.

A. ineffectuality

B. prowess

C. hollowness

Situation 6

1. Generally, relatives or patients directly employ a nursing care attendant without adequate evaluative criteria to select the most <u>appropriate</u> care provider.

A. preposterous

B. malapropos

C. felicitous

2. Additionally, outsourcing firms lack objective criteria for selecting nursing care attendants, leading to <u>widespread</u> customer dissatisfaction and increasing management difficulty.

A. pandemic

B. circumscribed

C. terminable

3. Given the 22 hospital subsidized nursing homes and 18 respiratory care wards currently operating in Taiwan, the importance of nursing care attendants is <u>obvious</u>.

A. obscure

B. lucid

C. inconspicuous

4. The inability to manage effectively the quality of service that nursing care attendants provide will lead to a further decline in hospital revenues, and <u>eventually</u> to a reduction in personnel and community services.

A. ultimately

B. PDQ

C. pronto

5. Therefore, a selection model based on fuzzy theory and the AHP method must be developed, capable of providing an objective means of evaluating the quality of nursing care attendants and, ultimately, enhancing the quality of service, increasing customer <u>satisfaction</u> and lowering personnel costs.

A. vexation

B. envy

C. conciliation

Unit Two

Recommendation Reports

調查性與建議性報告

- Identify the objectives, methodology and anticipated results to solve the technical problem
  建議性報告告知讀者管理目標、方法論及預期的結果，以求解決特定的管理問題

- Describe the nature of the problem
  該解決的管理問題是什麼？

- Offer suggestions on how to solve the problem
  您的機構對解決問題有何提議？

- Outline the strategy to achieve the project goal
  您的機構計畫如何實行這個目標？

- Emphasize how the company would benefit from achieving the set goal(s).
  達成目標的立即利益為何？

- Summarize how the larger industry or field would benefit from achieving the project goal(s).
  達成目標後會對管理界其他人造成何種利益？

Vocabulary and related expressions

differentiated marketing practices	差異化行銷作法（實務）
complete customer profile	完整的客戶資料
customer ranking model	客戶排名模式
dynamic purchasing behavior	動態採購行為
data mining method	資料倉儲法
enhanced management model	提升的管理模式
social welfare policy	社會福利政策
forecast market trends	預測市場趨勢（潮流）
long-term healthcare resources	長期健保資源
significant amount of data	大量資料
proposed forecasting models	提議的預測模型
relevant policies and strategies	相關政策與策略
purchasing on credit	以賒欠（記帳）方式採購（採買）
defaulted loan burden	拖欠貸款的沉重壓力
overdraft records	透支紀錄
outstanding loans and income	待付貸款和收入
greatly facilitating the decision	大大有助於做出明智決策
pave the way for	為……舖出一條康莊大道
advanced aging society	高齡社會
long-term care residential communities	長期關心住宅社區
emerging growth sector	新興成長產業
satisfying consumer demand	滿足消費者需求
valuation standard	評估（估價）標準
increasingly competitive sector	逐漸競爭的產業
under the auspices of	在……贊助之下
conventional statistical methods	依照慣例採取的統計法
effective business management strategies	有效的商業管理策略
valuable clinical information	極富價值的臨床資訊
patient confidentiality	（維護）病人（患者）的隱私
public appraisal	被大眾評選為
unforeseeable circumstances	無法預測的狀況
inventory management practices	庫存管理實踐（作法）
supply chain strategy	供應鏈策略
questionable results	讓人質疑的結果
sales volume	銷售量
appropriate control measures	適當的控制措施

Situation 1

Situation 2

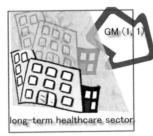

Situation 3

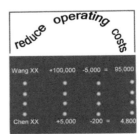

A Write down the key points of the situations on the preceding page, while the instructor reads aloud the script from the Answer Key. Alternatively, students can listen online at www.chineseowl.idv.tw.

Situation 1

_____

_____

_____

Situation 2

_____

_____

_____

Situation 3

_____

_____

_____

B Oral practice I

Based on the three situations in this unit, write three questions beginning with **What**, and answer them. The questions do not need to come directly from these situations.

Examples

What are conventional methods of ranking customers normally based on?

bank account balances in each accounting period

What prevents the provision of services specialized for individuals?

insufficient information on unique customer characteristics

1._____

_____

2._____

_____

3._____

_____

C Based on the three situations in this unit, write three questions beginning with **Why**, and answer them. The questions do not need to come directly from these situations.

Examples

Why has the demand for long-term healthcare facilities and services increased?

because of Taiwan's growing elderly population

Why do both governmental makers of social welfare policy and commercial investors rely heavily on forecasts?

to remain abreast of regulations that govern health financing and the development of new projects

1._____

_____

2._____

_____

3._____

_____

D Based on the three situations in this unit, write three questions beginning with **How**, and answer them. The questions do not need to come directly from these situations.

Examples

How has purchasing on credit become increasingly common in Taiwan?

owing to the rise in customer loans granted by local banks in recent years

How do banking officers often process loan applications?

by scoring a customer's credit rating based on a standard that lacks objectivity and requires considerable human resources to apply

1._____

_____

2._____

_____

3._____

_____

E Write questions that match the answers provided.

1._____

_____

to enhance the identification, acquisition and retention of loyal and profitable customers

2._____

_____

the modeling method

3._____

_____

other industrial applications

Listening Comprehension I

Situation 1

1. What could cause our company to lose its focus on product development and promotional strategies?

    A. the inability to understand the dynamic purchasing behavior of customers and identify those who have the potential to generate bank revenues

    B. the inability to interact compatibly with customers

    C. the inability to determine the customer's value in customer relationship management

2. Why is it impossible to provide services specialized for individuals?

    A. insufficient information on unique customer characteristics

    B. inability to devise diverse promotional strategies or customize products or services according to consumer needs

    C. the company's inability to attract new customers

3. How can one develop a customer ranking model?

    A. by enhancing the identification, acquisition and retention of loyal and profitable customers

    B. by providing a complete customer profile

    C. by analyzing the dynamic purchasing behavior of customers and identifying those who have the potential to generate bank revenues

4. What are conventional methods of ranking customers normally based on?

    A. types of products purchased, their quantity and their cost of acquisition and servicing

    B. bank account balances in each accounting period

    C. diverse promotional strategies or customized products or services

5. On what basis can one devise diverse promotional strategies or customize products or services?

A. the customer's value in customer relationship management

B. consumer needs

C. customer relationship management

Situation 2

1. Why do governmental makers of social welfare policy and commercial investors rely heavily on forecasts?

    A. to provide a valuable reference for makers of health-care policy, investors when devising relevant policies and strategies

    B. to remain abreast of regulations that govern health financing and the development of new projects

    C. to estimate the demand of the elderly population in Taiwan for the available long-term healthcare resources

2. What have most studies neglected?

    A. forecasting the medical market trends (both in supply and demand)

    B. forecasting market trends in long-term care in Taiwan

    C. the market and natural factors that affect the long-term healthcare sector

3. How can researchers collect the data of the study?

    A. by analyzing the relationship between the demand and critical factors

    B. using a questionnaire

    C. by measuring precisely the demand for and supply of long-term healthcare resources in Taiwan

4. What can the proposed forecasting models identify?

    A. factors that affect the demand

    B. a GM (1, 1) model based on Grey Theory

    C. the demand for and supply of long-term healthcare resources

5. How can researchers develop a multi-regression model in this study?

    A. by forecasting the supply of available long-term healthcare resources from data acquired from the website of Taiwan's Ministry of Interior

B. by measuring precisely the demand for and supply of long-term healthcare resources in Taiwan

C. by accumulating a significant amount of data and identifying such factors

Situation 3

1. When does the banking officer frequently score a customer's credit rating?

   A. when analyzing a mass volume of data

   B. when processing loan applications

   C. integrating customer data

2. What evidence suggests that purchasing on credit is increasingly common in Taiwan?

   A. the potential for data mining applications in financial institutions

   B. the rise in customer loans granted by local banks in recent years

   C. the trend to reduce the defaulted loan burden of small financial institutions

3. How can one devise a credit risk assessment model?

   A. by identifying the attributes of each customer account

   B. by establishing a database that integrates customer data

   C. by analyzing a mass volume of data or detecting concealed purchasing models

4. How can the credit risk assessment model reduce operating costs?

   A. by enhancing the process flow

   B. by paving the way for other potential data mining applications in financial institutions

   C. by greatly facilitating the decision of a banking officer regarding whether to grant a loan

5. Why does this study apply highly effective data mining approaches?

   A. to reduce the defaulted loan burden of small financial institutions

   B. to establish credit ranking criteria based on a decision tree

   C. to identify the attributes of each customer account

G Reading Comprehension I
Select the word or expression whose meaning is closest to the meaning of the underlined word or expression in the following passages.

Situation 1

1. Based on numerous available customer data, a data mining method, CRISP-DM, which combines the conventional means of data <u>exploration</u> with two mathematical calculations (decision tree and category nerve) can be adopted to determine how various purchasing activities are related and how many factors are involved in evaluating a customer's relationship.

   A. counterargument

   B. reconnaissance

   C. rejoinder

2. These factors include the types of products purchased, their quantity and their cost of <u>acquisition</u> and servicing.

   A. patronage

   B. procurement

   C. benefaction

3. Factors associated with customer relations and customer life cycle can then be combined to construct an enhanced management model. In the proposed model, factors of the ranking module are verified and adjusted to ensure that a company <u>continuously</u> provides quality services.

   A. perpetually

   B. intermittently

   C. sporadically

4. The customer's value in customer relationship management can be determined, and the model significantly enhances the company's ability to <u>attract</u> new

customers.

A. cold shoulder

B. rebuff

C. solicit

5. Furthermore, this model can be used in other business sectors to enhance the identification, acquisition and retention of loyal and <u>profitable</u> customers.

A. lucrative

B. defunct

C. sterile

Situation 2

1. A multi-regression model can be developed to measure and forecast not only the quantity of early demand, but also the relationship between the demand and critical factors by <u>accumulating</u> a significant amount of data and identifying such factors.

A. repudiating

B. abjuring

C. compiling

2. The data can then be <u>collected</u> using a questionnaire, with the factors quantitatively measured using a method found in the literature.

A. doled out

B. amassed

C. disseminated

3. Next, a GM (1, 1) model based on Grey Theory can be developed to accurately forecast the supply of available long-term healthcare resources from data <u>acquired</u> from the website of Taiwan's Ministry of Interior.

A. forfeited

B. wangled

C. relinquished

4. In addition to identifying factors that affect the demand, the proposed forecasting models can also measure <u>precisely</u> the demand for and supply of long-term healthcare resources in Taiwan.

   A. smack-dab

   B. surmised

   C. guesstimated

5. The proposed forecasting models provide a valuable reference for makers of health-care policy, investors in the medical sector, administrators and academics, when <u>devising</u> relevant policies and strategies.

   A. concocting

   B. obliterating

   C. liquidating

Situation 3

1. Credit ranking criteria based on a decision tree can then be <u>established</u> for all customers in the bank's database.

   A. inculcated

   B. abrogated

   C. negated

2. In addition to greatly facilitating the decision of a banking officer regarding whether to grant a loan, the credit risk assessment model can reduce operating costs by <u>enhancing</u> the process flow.

   A. depreciating

   B. aggrandizing

   C. abating

3. Moreover, the proposed model can pave the way for other potential data mining applications in financial institutions, such as more <u>effective</u> marketing

strategies.

A. nugatory

B. futile

C. emphatic

4. Moreover, the proposed model can <u>pave the way for</u> other potential data mining applications in financial institutions, such as more effective marketing strategies.

A. preclude

B. facilitate

C. impede

5. The proposed model is also very <u>promising</u> for other industrial applications.

A. propitious

B. inauspicious

C. foreboding

H　Common elements in writing a recommendation report 調查性與建議性報告 include the following.

a. 建議性報告告知讀者管理目標、方法論及預期的結果，以求解決特定的管理問題

範例 i

該解決的管理問題是什麼？

Recently emerging semiconductor technologies have ushered in the feasibility of embedding several digital modules in a printed-circuit board (PCB) and combining a larger system with several sub-chips. Moreover, the system clock operates at a higher frequency than conventional systems do. Under these circumstances, the clock-skew problem becomes a critical issue. Owing to different clock propagations, the sub-modules of a digital system may be asynchronous. The process, voltage, temperature, and loading (PVTL) factors inevitably induce the clock-skew problem. Moreover, the skew problem will worsen as the clock' operational frequency increases, becoming a bottleneck in future-high-performance systems and possibly resulting in system malfunctioning.

範例 ii

3D models are extensively adopted in multimedia applications owing to their relatively low cost and the ease with which they construct animated 3D objects. Although considerable effort has been paid to developing a concise and relatively easy means of constructing 3D faces, animating a human face is still extremely difficult. In particular, conventional 3D models are too time consuming and inaccurate when constructing digital objects since they manually retrieve 2D images.

b. 您的機構對解決問題有何提議？

範例 i

Therefore, we recommend developing a SAR-controlled DLL deskew circuit scheme, capable of reducing the system clock skew problem.

範例 ii

Therefore, we recommend developing develop an efficient face model that can formulate the 3D image of an individual's face from three 2D images.

c. 您的機構計畫如何實行這個目標？

範例 i

To do so, SAR can be used to control the DLL so that the deskew circuit can be automatically optimized for clock synchronization. The SAR binary search method can then be adopted to reduce the lock time and maintain tight synchronization. Next, with the clock-deskew buffers' using inverter chains, the deskew circuit can reduce the system clock skew and obtain a perfect output clock duty cycle. Additionally, the delay buffer chain can be adjusted so that the deskew circuit can fit in different operating environments. Finally, the architecture can be implemented using Synopsys and Cadence tools

範例 ii

To do so, three 2D images can be obtained simultaneously with three general cameras. The images can then be transferred to a personal computer. Next, the proposed model can be used to formulate digitally the 3D face.

d. 達成目標的立即利益為何？

範例 i

As anticipated, the proposed scheme can reduce the number of locking cycles in the system clock more efficiently than the conventional approaches can.

範例 ii

As anticipated, the proposed face model can reduce the time to construct a 3D face by 10% through optimizing the 3D model rather than manually retrieving 2D images. Additionally, the proposed model can precisely formulate an individual's face by using conventional peripheral equipment. Moreover, the constructed 3D face can not only be sculptured by automatic machinery, but can also simulate various expressions. The equipment required for constructing 3D digital objects includes three cameras, a personal computer, and common image software. Furthermore, steps to construct 3D digital objects in the proposed face model are simplified, reducing the related formulation costs and time to use the optimization methods.

e. 達成目標後會對管理界其他人造成何種利益？

範例 i

The proposed scheme proposed to develop an SAR-controlled DLL deskew circuit can reduce the system clock-skew and achieve a perfect output clock duty cycle. Furthermore, the deskew circuit can eliminate system malfunctioning caused by the clock skew problem. Only the development of a deskew circuit can allow the system clock to operate at Giga Hertz without interference.

範例 ii

Importantly, the proposed face model can minimize the tolerable errors associated with constructing a digital face, enhancing multimedia or animation applications by reducing formulation costs and creating more realistic digital objects. The proposed model can be employed to digitize different real 3D objects.

In the space below, write a recommendation report.

_____

_____

_____

_____

_____

_____

_____

_____

_____

_____

Recommendation Reports
調查性與建議性報告

Look at the following examples of a recommendation report.

範例 i

該解決的管理問題是什麼？ Piecewise linearization algorithms are extensively used in nonlinear programming. For instance, trading companies attempt to minimize the costs of factory-vendor transportation and ordering transactions. Such scenarios are normally formulated in a nonlinear format. Conventional algorithms can only obtain a local optimum in such scenarios. However, the difference between local and global optima leads to unexpected costs. Still, piecewise linearization algorithms require too much time to obtain an optimum solution. For instance, while the objective function or constraint of a nonlinear problem is highly nonlinear, the solution and performance is always inadequate. 您的機構對解決問題有何提議？ Therefore, we recommend developing an enhanced piecewise linearization algorithm, capable of obtaining the global optimum of a nonlinear model, for use in a web based optimization system. 您的機構計畫如何實行這個目標？ To do so, a web-based optimization system can be implemented based on the enhanced algorithm and using a dynamic linking library procedure. The system can then be linked to many other mathematical methods, for example, LINGO, to solve a nonlinear problem by integrating concurrent methods. Next, user specified problems can be stored in a database storage system. Additionally, the solution can be derived to guarantee the global optimum with an acceptable error rate. 達成目標的立即利益為何？ As anticipated, the enhanced piecewise linearization algorithm can reduce the computational time required to solve a nonlinear programming model to 50% of that required by piecewise linearization algorithms. Such an improvement not only significantly reduces computational time, but also allows users to make more efficient decisions. Moreover, the enhanced piecewise linearization algorithm can obtain the global optimum in general nonlinear programming models within a tolerable error and significantly increase computational efficiency by decreasing the use of 0-1 variables. 達成目標後會對管理界其他人造成何種利益？ In addition to its usefulness in obtaining the optimum solutions in fields such as medicine, biology and science, the proposed algorithm can also provide the global optimum with a tolerable error. Furthermore, through the web-based optimization system proposed herein, user-specified problems can be stored in a database and used repeatedly. Via the proposed web-based system, the enhanced piecewise linearization algorithm can be applied in diverse fields such as medicine, biology and engineering. Through the user-friendly interface of the web-based system, users can easily and efficiently input their nonlinear model.

範例 ii

該解決的管理問題是什麼？ Decision-making environments are increasingly complex. For instance, selecting the criteria for developing a decision evaluation model is extremely difficult. While the inclusion of too few criteria in the evaluation model leads to incomplete results, too many makes the model too complex and difficult to evaluate. Notably, conventional evaluation models are generally concerned only with economic factors and neglect factors that cannot be evaluated in money. However, large investment programs involve many intangible factors that cannot be valued, such as the satisfaction of related groups and potential environmental impact. 您的機構對解決問題有何提議？ Therefore, we recommend developing an efficient evaluation model capable of selecting natural gas bus brands. This model allows us to evaluate an appropriate number of criteria for cost and effectiveness. 您的機構計畫如何實行這個目標？ To do so, natural gas bus brands can be selected by the model based on cost effectiveness analysis. Two methodologies of multiple attribute decision making (MADM), including the technique for order preference by similarity to ideal solution (TOPSIS) and the analytic hierarchy process (AHP), can then be used to rank all viable alternatives to bus systems from a complete perspective. 達成目標的立即利益爲何？ As anticipated, the proposed model can evaluate exactly the relationship between the cost and effectiveness of all viable alternatives to bus systems. The evaluation results can provide not only economic information on all viable alternatives to bus systems, but also many other comparable situations. 達成目標後會對管理界其他人造成何種利益？ Importantly, the proposed model can provide a valuable reference for government when selecting brands of bus systems. The ranking methodology can provide a more objective outcome with weights of related decision groups, than can other methodologies. The ranking methodology can also provide a more flexible procedure with respect to the outcome's complexity. Moreover, the ranking outcome can allow decision makers to identify the order preferences for alternatives.

Situation 4

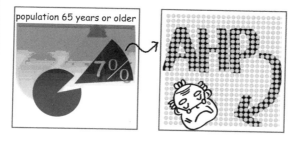
population 65 years or older
7%

successful operation

Situation 5

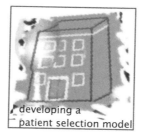

developing a patient selection model

questionnaire
customer satisfaction

Situation 6

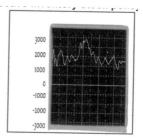
(S , R)

I Write down the key points of the situations on the preceding page, while the instructor reads aloud the script from the Answer Key. Alternatively, students can listen online at www.chineseowl.idv.tw.

Situation 4

_____

_____

_____

Situation 5

_____

_____

_____

Situation 6

_____

_____

_____

J Oral practice II
Based on the three situations in this unit, write three questions beginning with **Which**, and answer them. The questions do not need to come directly from these situations.

Examples

Which organization defined Taiwan as an advanced aging society as of the end of 1993?

the World Health Organization

Which factor explains growing concern over the market demand for long-term care residential communities?

aging in Taiwan

1._____

_____

2._____

_____

3._____

_____

K Based on the three situations in this unit, write three questions beginning with **What**, and answer them. The questions do not need to come directly from these situations.

Examples

What has Taiwan's National Health Insurance scheme strived to provide since its establishment in 1995?

medical coverage for all of the island's residents under the auspices of the National Health Insurance Bureau

What do hospitals often have difficulty in doing despite the high quality of the medical care provided?

understanding customer's needs

1. _____

_____

2. _____

_____

3. _____

_____

L Based on the three situations in this unit, write three questions beginning with *Why* and answer them. The questions do not need to come directly from these situations.

Examples

Why must enterprises adopt effective inventory management practices?

to improve their competitive edge

Why is an effective stock inventory system essential?

because inventory stock is often regarded as a somewhat static resource with economic value, and the quality of its management directly affects company operations.

1._____

_____

2._____

_____

3._____

_____

M Write questions that match the answers provided.

1._____

_____

to select the most appropriate sampling method

2._____

_____

conventional statistical methods such as AHP and TOPSIS

3._____

_____

to reduce the minimum stock that must be carried

N Listening Comprehension II

Situation 4

1. What percentage of the population 65 years or older comprises an advanced aging society?

   A. 4%

   B. 7%

   C. 15%

2. What have few long-term care studies attempted to identify?

   A. success factors in managing residential communities of senior citizens

   B. the market demand for long-term care residential communities

   C. the success of certain management practices in satisfying consumer demand

3. What can the AHP-based method enable administrators of senior citizen residential communities to do?

   A. select the most appropriate sampling method

   B. select the most feasible residential community during decision making

   C. identify critical factors for successful operations

4. How can one derive a valuation standard that reflects enterprise values?

   A. based on interviews with experts in the field

   B. based on a questionnaire survey

   C. the most appropriate sampling method

5. How can the proposed method enhance the competency of administrators?

   A. in satisfying consumer demand in this growing market sector

   B. in investing in this emerging growth sector

   C. in making their residential communities efficient

Situation 5

1. What do hospitals often have difficulty in doing?

A. understanding customer's needs

B. establishing effective business management strategies

C. gaining the confidence of patients in the quality of medical services

2. Why is it extremely difficult for hospitals to establish effective business management strategies?

A. owing to the difficulty in enhancing the public image of the hospital and increasing the current market demand for specific services

B. owing to the difficulty in gaining the confidence of patients in the quality of medical services

C. because conventional statistical methods such as AHP and TOPSIS cannot analyze how patients select a hospital for treatment, making extremely difficult the establishment of effective business management strategies

3. How is it possible to gain the confidence of patients in the quality of medical services?

A. by designing a framing questionnaire based on the basic requirements of patients

B. by analyzing incoming hospital patients in relation to public image of the hospital and the current market demand for specific services

C. by generating revenues independently of the national health insurance scheme

4. What does not necessarily improve customer satisfaction?

A. Taiwan's National Health Insurance scheme

B. medical coverage for all of the island's residents

C. the quality of hospital services

5. What influences the expectations of hospital patients?

A. the quality of service

B. public appraisal of the quality of medical treatment

C. patients' demands

Situation 6

1. How can enterprises improve their competitive edge?

   A. by understanding how the quality of its management directly affects their operations

   B. by adopting effective inventory management practices

   C. by focusing on specific stock inventory systems

2. What do previous studies focus on?

   A. the supply chain strategy for a stock inventory of multiple products with many suppliers

   B. establishing inventory stock management policies

   C. specific stock inventory systems

3. Why is simulation inefficient and yields questionable results?

   A. It requires much time.

   B. It is too complex.

   C. It requires the use of other statistical methods.

4. How can one utilize the stock model (s , Q)?

   A. to determine the inventory stock cost, sales volume and orders in short supply

   B. to reduce overhead costs and enable enterprise managers to select the most effective inventory stock policy

   C. to derive the inventory stock models of the supplier and manufacturer without complex mathematics

5. How can the proposed management model determine precisely the supplier and the manufacturers?

   A. by using random and the most appropriate control measures

   B. by enabling enterprise managers to select the most effective inventory stock policy

   C. by adopting the most appropriate control channel

O Reading Comprehension II
Select the word or expression whose meaning is closest to the meaning of the underlined word or expression in the following passages.

Situation 4

1. A valuation standard that reflects enterprise values can then be <u>derived</u> based on interviews with experts in the field.

   A. sundered

   B. excogitated

   C. severed

2. Next, <u>critical</u> factors for successful operations can be identified using the AHP method.

   A. pivotal

   B. piddling

   C. meager

3. The proposed AHP-based method can enable enterprises involved in the development of senior citizen residential communities to identify the features of and prerequisites for <u>successful</u> operations.

   A. foiled

   B. aborted

   C. efficacious

4. The proposed method can enable administrators of residential communities of senior citizens to select the most <u>feasible</u> residential community during decision making by considering financial and market-related concerns to ensure the success of daily operations.

   A. mind-boggling

   B. expedient

C. implausible

5. In addition to enhancing the competency of administrators in making their residential communities efficient in this increasingly <u>competitive</u> sector, the proposed method can provide a valuable reference for experts, academics and investors.

A. obsequious

B. cutthroat

C. demure

Situation 5

1. The following criterion can be applied to analyze the questionnaire results: physicians must be qualified and reliable; medical staff must have received sufficient training; physicians must be willing to offer valuable clinical information; physicians must express concern for their patients; medical staff must display a <u>professional</u> attitude; and hospital administration must respect patient confidentiality. SPSS software can be used to analyze the results.

A. dabbler

B. putterer

C. crackerjack

2. Moreover, the following four assumptions are made. Public appraisal of the quality of medical treatment affects the overall results; the quality of service influences the expectations of hospital patients; patients' demands influence the quality of service, and a patient's experience influences the <u>expected</u> quality of service.

A. inferred

B. prodigious

C. fortuitous

3. The proposed patient selection model is established using AHP and TOPSIS,

since conventional statistical models are <u>useless</u>.

A. pragmatic

B. utilitarian

C. ineffectual

4. While influencing which hospital that a patient selects, the quality of hospital services does not <u>necessarily</u> improve customer satisfaction.

A. indubitably

B. gratuitous

C. extraneous

5. Moreover, the proposed model helps hospitals develop an effective strategy for generating revenues <u>independently</u> of the national health insurance scheme.

A. expedited

B. abetted

C. autonomously

Situation 6

1. Problems encountered by the supplier and the manufacturer in predicting the required amount of inventory stock can be <u>addressed</u>.

A. shunned

B. overlooked

C. pontificated

2. The stock model (s , Q) can be utilized to derive the inventory stock models of the supplier and manufacturer without <u>complex</u> mathematics.

A. mosaic

B. self-explanatory

C. turkey shoot

3. The supplier and the manufacturer can adopt the most <u>appropriate</u> control channel to determine the inventory stock cost, sales volume and orders in short

supply.

A. incongruous

B. antithetical

C. pertinent

4. The proposed inventory management model can determine the most economic time to <u>purchase</u> and inventory stock policy for both the supplier and the manufacturer.

A. hawk

B. patronize

C. peddle

5. By using <u>random</u> and the most appropriate control measures, the proposed management model can determine precisely the supplier and the manufacturers, reduce overhead costs and enable enterprise managers to select the most effective inventory stock policy.

A. contingent

B. painstaking

C. well-ordered

Unit Three

Persuasive Reports
說服力的展現

- Cite a statistic or recent trend to attract the readers' interest in a particular topic
  引起讀者注意

- Describe how the reader's interests are addressed in the project planning and strategy, as well as in customer service
  建立讀者對計畫、策略或服務的需求

- Discuss the feasibility of project success in terms of methodology, strategy and customer service
  展示計畫、策略或服務的可行性

- Highlight the anticipated benefits of project success
  引導讀者預想計畫、策略或服務實行後的成果

- Summarize the steps needed to ensure project success
  最後採取特定行動

Vocabulary and related expressions

rapidly evolve	迅速捲入
contrast with	與……相比之下
conventional marketing	墨守成規的行銷作法
consumer preferences	消費者的喜好（偏愛）
product innovation	產品革命（革新、變革）
behavioral patterns	行為模式
complex administrative procedures	複雜的管理程序（管理流程)
errors in insurance claims	保險索賠發生失誤（錯誤）
claimant errors	索賠者的失誤（錯誤）
National Health Insurance holders	全民健康保險的投保人
heavy daily workload	平日沉重的工作量
customer confidentiality	客戶隱私（機密）
implement separate frameworks	分開施行準則
compensate for this limitation	賠償（補償）這項限制
feasible forecasting method	可實施的預測法
health care expenditures	健康照護開銷（開支）
seek one's authorization	爭取某人的授權
budget deficits	預算赤字
concentration their effort on	他們群策群力……
customer retention	保留客戶
pertinent literature	相關文獻
feasible strategies	可實施的策略
healthcare managers	醫療保健部門經理
increasingly elderly population	年紀愈來愈大的人口
long-term care market	長期照護市場
social welfare trends	社會福利趨勢
expert conjecture	專家推測
institutional managers	機構的專業經理
feasible health care policy strategy	可施行的醫療保健政策策略
common business practices	普遍通行的商業作法（商業慣例）
credit rating status	信用評等境況
exacerbation	惡化；激怒；情況加劇惡化
stockholder profits	股東盈餘
small- and medium-sized enterprises	中小企業
lower administrative expenses	較低的行政管理開銷

Situation 1

Situation 2

Situation 3

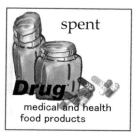

A Write down the key points of the situations on the preceding page, while the instructor reads aloud the script from the Answer Key. Alternatively, students can listen online at www.chineseowl.idv.tw.

Situation 1

_____

_____

_____

Situation 2

_____

_____

_____

Situation 3

_____

_____

_____

B Oral practice I
Based on the three situations in this unit, write three questions beginning with **Why**, and answer them. The questions do not need to come directly from these situations.

Examples

Why have marketing efforts in the local cosmetics sector increased?

because Taiwan's biotechnology industry has rapidly evolved in recent years

Why can a wide array of cosmetic brands be found in the marketplace?

because many female consumers regard cosmetics as a daily necessity

1._____

_____

2._____

_____

3._____

_____

C Based on the three situations in this unit, write three questions beginning with **What**, and answer them. The questions do not need to come directly from these situations.

Examples

What would cause NHI staff to spend much time in correcting errors and requesting insurers and claimants to amend erroneous information?

errors made due to confusion over the forms

What would adhering to all NHI regulations require?

filling out more than 30 forms

1._____

_____

2._____

_____

3._____

_____

D Based on the three situations in this unit, write three questions beginning with **How**, and answer them. The questions do not need to come directly from these situations.

Examples

How are customers allowed to purchase a wide range of medical and health food products?

by local pharmacies that have adopted a business model of one-stop shopping in recent years

How are managers almost prevented from analyzing market competition accurately and developing effective strategies?

owing to the inability to accurately forecast the share household consumption spent on medical and health care, or the number of local pharmacies to be established

1._____

_____

2._____

_____

3._____

_____

E Write questions that match the answers provided.

1._____

_____

the Industrial Technology Research Institute

2._____

_____

the literature

3._____

_____

since 1997

F Listening Comprehension I

Situation 1

1. Why are marketing efforts increasing in the local cosmetics sector?

   A. because Taiwan's biotechnology industry has rapidly evolved in recent years

   B. because revenues in the local cosmetics sector ranged between US$ 1.7 billion and US$ 1.8 billion in 2002

   C. because many industrialized countries are affected by the globalization of the cosmetics sector

2. How is the wide array of cosmetic brands reflected in the marketplace?

   A. by the enormous female consumer demand and intense competition

   B. by the fact that the cosmetics sector originally focused only on healthcare products

   C. by the fact that many female consumers regard cosmetics as a daily necessity

3. What factors necessitate that manufacturers must better understand consumer purchasing behavior in this market niche?

   A. operating costs and enhanced competitiveness

   B. enormous female consumer demand and intense competition

   C. marketing practices and the potential lowering of product and service quality

4. What enables local cosmetic manufacturers to increase their share of the market in related products and services?

   A. Industrial Technology Research Institute

   B. A questionnaire submitted to cosmetics manufacturers on the most appropriate marketing method

   C. adopting this 4P-based marketing strategy

5. In what area will the 4P-based marketing strategy provide Taiwan's biotech industry with clear guidelines?

   A. for equipping management in the local cosmetics sector with appropriate and efficient marketing policies

B. for potentially lowering product and service quality

C. for increasing productivity and lowering overhead

Situation 2

1. Why have errors in insurance claims and much inefficiency occurred in Taiwan's National Health Insurance (NHI) scheme?

    A. confusion over the forms to be filed

    B. complex administrative procedures

    C. redundancy of forms to be filed

2. How many forms must be filled out to adhere to all NHI regulations?

    A. more than 30

    B. more than 25

    C. more than 40

3. What creates substantial overhead and requires additional time to be spent?

    A. inability to streamline the processing of insurance premiums and other insurance-related claims

    B. use of telephone, fax or mail to correct NHI form-related errors

    C. slow access to relevant customer data online

4. Why is simplifying NHI forms and procedures a priority?

    A. because of the limited number of available staff

    B. because of the amount of human resources involved in handling insurer and claimant errors

    C. because of the amount of time required to fill out insurance claims and the postage fees

5. Why is the smooth flow of operations especially important?

    A. because of insurer and claimant errors

    B. because of administrative costs and the number of personnel involved

C. because of the extremely heavy daily workload

Situation 3

1. Why have over-the-counter drug purchases, along with sanitary and other related medical products, become major revenue generators for pharmacies?

   A. because local pharmacies have adopted a business model of one-stop shopping in recent years

   B. because the Taiwanese government has been implementing separate frameworks for the medical and pharmaceutical sectors

   C. because the rate of filling of hospital prescription drugs by pharmacies is extremely low

2. Why are customers allowed to purchase a wide range of medical and health food products?

   A. because the Taiwanese government has been implementing separate frameworks for the medical and pharmaceutical sectors

   B. because local pharmacies have adopted a business model of one-stop shopping in recent years

   C. because the number of local pharmacies to be established almost prevents managers from analyzing market competition accurately and developing effective strategies

3. Why are managers almost prevented from analyzing market competition accurately and developing effective strategies?

   A. owing to the inability to compensate for the number of local pharmacies to be established

   B. owing to the inability to accurately forecast the share household consumption spent on medical and health care

   C. owing to the inability to identify how the share of household consumption on medical and health care is related to the number of pharmacies

4. How can the proposed method provide a valuable reference for governmental authorities?

A. when formulating policies

B. when developing competitive marketing strategies

C. when estimating the growth of medical and health care expenditures

5. How long has the Taiwanese government been implementing separate frameworks for the medical and pharmaceutical sectors?

A. since 1998

B. since 1996

C. since 1997

G Reading Comprehension I
Select the word or expression whose meaning is closest to the meaning of the underlined word or expression in the following passages.

Situation 1

1. Adopting this 4P-based marketing strategy enables local cosmetic manufacturers to increase their <u>share</u> of the market in related products and services.

   A. nihility

   B. allotment

   C. vacuum

2. The proposed strategy also helps planners to make decisions more objectively than is supported by conventional approaches, ultimately <u>accelerating</u> the effectiveness of the marketing process.

   A. impeding

   B. revving up

   C. retarding

3. In addition to encouraging product innovation, the 4P-based marketing strategy provides Taiwan's biotech industry with <u>clear</u> guidelines for equipping management in the local cosmetics sector with appropriate and efficient marketing policies that will ultimately reduce operating costs and enhance competitiveness.

   A. halcyon

   B. dismal

   C. sullen

4. The proposed method also reveals how the biotechnology industry can incorporate 4P concepts to <u>clarify</u> the behavioral patterns of cosmetics

customers.

A. delineate

B. obfuscate

C. muddle

5. We seek your <u>prompt</u> approval of the implementation of this novel marketing strategy in your organization so that you can more easily understand the behavioral patterns of your cosmetics customers.

A. torpid

B. instantaneous

C. dilatory

Situation 2

1. The proposed administrative procedure <u>streamlines</u> the filing insurance-related claims by simplifying the forms and enabling efficient access to relevant customer data online.

A. disbands

B. amalgamates

C. strews

2. Importantly, the proposed procedure significantly reduces not only the amount of time required to fill out insurance <u>claims</u>, but also the postage fees.

A. requisitions

B. abjurations

C. renunciations

3. The network-based system <u>accelerates</u> data processing.

A. thwarts

B. stymies

C. precipitates

4. This highly restricted networked-based system that ensures NHI customer

confidentiality is unique in that it not only integrates the efforts of various organizations within the NHI scheme by providing data access, but also makes NHI administrative services more <u>flexible</u> for customers.

A. malleable

B. indomitable

C. adamant

5. We therefore strongly <u>recommend</u> that you adopt this administrative procedure to streamline the processing of insurance premiums and other insurance-related claims in Taiwan's National Health Insurance (NHI) scheme.

A. vex

B. deprecate

C. extol

Situation 3

1. Based on these data, the GM (1, N) model of the Grey theory is applied for <u>forecasting</u> purposes.

A. reminiscing

B. rehashing

C. prognosticating

2. The proposed forecasting method can accurately estimate medical and health care expenditures as well as the number of pharmacies to be <u>established</u> in Taiwan from 2008 to 2010.

A. expunged

B. vacated

C. inculcated

3. The proposed method can also <u>identify</u> how the share of household consumption on medical and health care is related to the number of pharmacies.

A. pettifog

B. peg

C. double-talk

4. Importantly, the proposed method provides a valuable reference for both governmental authorities in <u>formulating</u> policies and pharmaceutical managers in developing competitive marketing strategies.

A. scrambling

B. concocting

C. ruffling

5. We therefore seek your authorization to adopt this forecasting method to ensure that an adequate number of pharmacies, located strategically, can <u>meet</u> health consumer demand in Taiwan.

A. rebuff

B. rebuke

C. comply with

H Common elements in writing a persuasive report 說服力 的展現 include the following.

a. 引起讀者注意：描述一個事實或情勢跟管理類的讀者所關心的特定情 勢做連結。

範例 i

Although adopted in solving problems related to ordered categorical data, statistical methods are rarely applied to problems related to ordered categorical data quality. In addition to the accumulated analysis method (AA method) proposed by Taguchi, similar scored methods have also been proposed to solve problems of quality. Owing to its emphasis on the location effect, the AA method can accurately estimate only the location effect. To compensate for the limitations of the AA method, other scored methods have been proposed to accurately estimate the dispersion effect.

範例 ii

The build to order (BTO) model is gradually replacing the build to forecast (BTF) model. Process quality and delivery time have been increasingly emphasized by the highly competitive electronics industry. Additionally, many statisticians and engineers such as Kane, Kotz, and Pearn *et al.* have proposed process capability indices (PCIs) to assess the effectiveness of a process.

b. 建立讀者對計畫、策略或服務的需求：描述管理問題和需求間的連帶 關係，以及不解決問題的後果。

範例 i

Despite their extensive use in solving problems related to ordered categorical data quality, the AA method and conventional scored methods are unnecessarily complex and inaccurate, confounding the location and dispersion effects. Their implementation leads to an inaccurate optimal combination of process parameters, thus requiring much time and a higher cost in the product design stage.

範例 ii

Although performance has received considerable attention and many evaluation methods have been developed, manufacturing and delivery time have seldom been discussed. Additionally, conventional process capability indices (PCIs) can neither objectively assess quality and delivery time nor identify the relationship between PCIs and the conformation rate of DT and OCT. Utilizing point estimators of the PCIs is generally an inaccurate means of estimating the real PCIs for suppliers. Therefore, the lack of an effective performance index and an objective testing procedure will lead to inefficiency and a high overhead cost. Furthermore, if firms do not perform well in terms of quality and delivery, they will lose their market competitiveness. The outcome will also delay the firms' production.

c. 展示計畫、策略或服務的可行性：詳細描述完成計畫或策略目標的必須步驟。

範例 i

To resolve this problem, we have developed an efficient response surface methodology capable of optimizing ordered categorical data process parameters, since setting the process parameters leads to optimization of the location and dispersion effects. This novel method with simplified calculations of the mean and standard deviation of ordered categorical responses is used to estimate the location and dispersion effects. Additionally, regression models are used to relate the location and dispersion effects to the controlled factor levels. An optimal combination of process parameters is also obtained using the dual response surface methodology.

範例 ii

Therefore, we have developed an effective performance index (PCI) and develop an objective hypothesis testing procedure for PCIs, capable of assessing the operational cycle time (OCT) and delivery time (DT) for VLSI. A quality performance index is also used to assess operational cycle time and delivery time of VLSI.

d. 引導讀者預想計畫、策略或服務實行後的成果：強調採行該計畫或策略後立即和長期的利益。

範例 i

As anticipated, the proposed method with calculations of the mean and standard deviation of ordered categorical responses can accurately estimate the location and dispersion effects. In addition, the method can be easily implemented and the location effect clearly separated from the dispersion effect. The dual response surface methodology can be used to obtain an optimal combination of process parameters and help engineers set the controlled factors, and alleviate the quality problem related to ordered categorical data. To do so, the PCIs of OCT and DT are defined and, then, the UMVU (uniformly minimum variance) estimators of the studied PCIs are derived under the assumption of a normal distribution. Next, the above estimators are used to construct the one-to-one relationship between the PCIs and the conforming rate of DT (or OCT). Finally, a hypothesis testing procedure for PCIs is developed.

範例 ii

As anticipated, this hypothesis testing procedure allows firms to assess the performance indices of the operation cycle time (OCT) and delivery time (DT) of VLSI, increasing the competitiveness of suppliers. Based on these performance indices, the corresponding tables of the excess time limit rate of OCT are also provided for manufacturing VLSI and DT, based on a supplier's schedule. These tables confirm the required performance index (PCI) value for manufacturers. Moreover, the hypothesis testing procedure for performance index is adopted to assess whether the OCT and DT satisfies the firm's requirements. Importantly, this work can provide a procedure for testing PCIs of OCT (DT) and a corresponding table of PCIs versus conforming rates of DT and OCT for suppliers. In addition to investigating the operational cycle time (OCT) of an individual manufacturing step for VLSI, the testing procedure can be used to assess the delivery time to satisfy customer requirements.

e. 最後採取特定行動：管理類的讀者經由完成計畫或策略來有效貢獻管理部門中的特定領域。

範例 i

We seek your expedient approval to implement this novel procedure in your daily administrative operations in order to increase work productivity.

範例 ii

We therefore highly recommend that your quality assurance department adopt this performance index (PCI) and objective hypothesis testing procedure to accelerate product testing during VLSI manufacturing, ultimately increasing customer satisfaction owing to accelerated product delivery.

In the space below, write a persuasive report.

_____

_____

_____

_____

_____

_____

_____

_____

_____

_____

Look at the following examples of a persuasive report.

範例 i

引起讀者注意 Geographic-based information is increasingly used in daily living. There is always the need to know, "Where am I going to?" and, "How do I get there?" in cases such as visiting a friend, going somewhere for business, sightseeing, making holiday plans, and so on. The required geographic information may be as simple an address, or as complicated as the complete path and estimation of time. Many kinds of geographical information are needed for various purposes. Many convenient applications that provide such information on PDAs are available in the market today. An increasing number of consumers use these applications. 建立讀者對計畫、策略或服務的需求 However, the passive mode of accessing information fails to transmit effectively geographic-based information to PDA users. Users cannot use the system all the time, but some critical geographic-related information may appear when users are busy on other tasks. In some cases, they need to be informed immediately. If they have answers on time, they may save time, resolve an emergency, or even avoid an accident. However, no system capable of actively paging users exists. The inability of PDA users to receive updated information in a timely manner will limit PDA use to within a narrow range. Such a limitation may discourage PDA use. Most people will not buy such an expensive "notepad" when they don't think its functions are useful . Only the evidently useful and convenient functions may change people's life styles and become essential. The conventional GIS systems in PDAs are not so advantageous as to be "killer applications" .

展示計畫、策略或服務的可行性 Therefore, we have designed a GIS-based architecture that supports an automatic reporting service through handheld mobile devices. To do so, the coordinates of a PDA user are obtained by using a GPS module. These coordinates are then transmitted to the back-end server through a wireless network and used as the filter to query the database. Next, query results are sent back to the PDA, triggering an event to inform the PDA user. 引導讀者預想計畫、策略或服務實行後的成果 As anticipated, the GIS-based architecture can automatically page PDA users through a wireless network when desired local information becomes available. Using the global positioning system (GPS) feature, the system will periodically send the position of the use to the server. The server will then check for any local news about disasters or roadblocks, and for advertisements. The results will be sent back to the user's machine and an event triggered to remind the user. Importantly, the GIS-based architecture can allow PDA users to access information with their geographic position's functioning as a filter. This avoids sending too much junk information to users. Limited by bandwidth and the speed of wireless network, this study also design strategies for data storage that involve a robust multi-tier architecture. The many geographic data are placed on the server, and only required data are transferred to the client host through the network. 最後採取特定行動 We therefore highly recommend that you adopt this GIS-based architecture in your company's mobile communication devices to effectively respond to constantly changing consumer trends and preferences.

範例 ii

引起讀者注意 As is well known, ionizing irradiation incurs material damage. The range/number of radiation effects in solids depends on both crystal structure and the type of ionizing irradiation. Additionally, the energy and dosage of irradiation essentially affect radiation processes. Ionizing irradiation excites both electronic and ionic subsystems of crystals. Relaxation processes occur after excitation, forming defects. Defects impair the solids, extensively stimulating material damage. However, the radiation-stimulated ordering effect (RSOE) is found in various materials. At least two competitive processes are observed in crystals and semiconductors under ionizing irradiation - 1) generation of radiation defects and 2) radiation-stimulated annihilation of defects. On a specific stage,

95

the annihilation of irradiation defects can dominate the generation of defects, enhancing the structure. This stage is referred to as RSOE. Therefore, low-dose irradiation could serve as an effective method for increasing the reliability of semiconductors and the stability of parameters in the final stage of manufacturing. This fact substantially increases economical efficiency. 建立讀者對計畫、策略或服務的需求 Nevertheless, the RSOE mechanisms in II-VI semiconductors remain unknown, making it impossible to implement process applications capable of increasing the efficiency of barrier structures. Although the application of RSOE could markedly increase product output in microelectronics, the generalization and analysis of RSOE remain an obstacle to further development.

展示計畫、策略或服務的可行性 Therefore, we have investigated the RSOE mechanism in II-VI semiconductors and constructed a related model. To do so, voltage-current characteristics (VIC), voltage-capacity characteristics (VCC) and capacity-modulated spectra for barrier structures are determined at various irradiation doses, providing the preliminary experimental data. Based on that data, the control parameters are then derived. Following Hall experiments to consider bulk effects, the parametric changes are analyzed and synthesized. 引導讀者預想計畫、策略或服務實行後的成果 Low-dose radiation processes can be clarified in solids, improving the parameters of structures based on II-VI semiconductors. The proposed work can also elucidate low-dose radiation processes in II-VI semiconductors.. Thus, applying this model to barrier structure manufacturing allows us to predict accurately the irradiation conditions to enhance the parameters of structures based on II-VI semiconductors. Importantly, the range of objects in which the RSOE is observed can be expanded. II-VI and other (Si, III-V) semiconductors can also be compared in terms of the RSOE mechanisms. Analysis of RSOE in II-VI reveals the peculiarities of related objects. In contrast to III-V semiconductors, for which the properties of "pure" crystals are determined by impurities in II-VI semiconductors, the lattice "stoichiometric" defects prevails. Naturally, RSOE can be explained by the reconstruction of defect centers. Importantly, the proposed model considers the effect of the radiation-stimulated diffusion (RSD) of point defects. 最後採取特定行動 We therefore seek your authorization to continue with our investigations of RSOE mechanisms in II-VI semiconductors, ultimately contributing to the economic competitiveness of our country's semiconductor manufacturing sector.

Situation 4

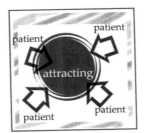

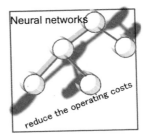

Situation 5

Situation 6

I Write down the key points of the situations on the preceding page, while the instructor reads aloud the script from the Answer Key. Alternatively, students can listen online at www.chineseowl.idv.tw.

Situation 4

_____

_____

_____

Situation 5

_____

_____

_____

Situation 6

_____

_____

_____

Oral practice II
Based on the three situations in this unit, write three questions beginning with **Why**, and answer them. The questions do not need to come directly from these situations.

Examples

Why was a Global Budget System implemented in Taiwan? because of the extremely competitive medical market sector and budget deficits associated with the island's National Health Insurance scheme

Why do hospitals face considerable expenditure in attracting new patients? because they can not determine patient turnover rates precisely

1._____

_____

2._____

_____

3._____

_____

K Based on the three situations in this unit, write three questions beginning with **What**, and answer them. The questions do not need to come directly from these situations.

Examples

What must Taiwan effectively address?

the increasing demand for long-term healthcare facilities and services

What is a fundamental part of feasibility analysis?

forecasting (both supply and demand) trends in the long-term care market

1._____

_____

2._____

_____

3._____

_____

L Based on the three situations in this unit, write three questions beginning with **How** and answer them. The questions do not need to come directly from these situations.

Examples

How can one explain the often unknown credit rating status of most Taiwanese enterprises?

because they are small- and medium-sized

How have banks been able to reduce non-performing loans? by expending considerable time and human resources in diagnosing the ability of enterprises to repay loans

1._____

_____

2._____

_____

3._____

_____

M Write questions that match the answers provided.

1._____

_____

customer retention within the medical sector to increase a hospital's competitiveness

2._____

_____

the Ministry of Interior's website

3._____

_____

lending and investing

N Listening Comprehension II

Situation 4

1. How could one characterize the medical market sector in Taiwan?

   A. highly prioritized

   B. markedly improved

   C. extremely competitive

2. What are large budget deficits in Taiwan attributed to?

   A. implementation of a Global Budget System

   B. the island's National Health Insurance scheme

   C. a high patient turnover rate

3. Why do hospitals face considerable expenditure in attracting new patients?

   A. because they can not determine patient turnover rates precisely

   B. because they do not highly prioritize attracting new patients

   C. because they can not increase the operating costs of hospitals and lower the total number of patients

4. What has ultimately lowered the competitiveness of hospitals?

   A. a reduction in the operating costs of hospitals

   B. an increase in the total number of patients

   C. declining subsidies from the National Health Insurance scheme

5. How can hospitals provide high-quality and flexible health care services that will ultimately enhance their public image?

   A. by markedly improving relations with patients through use of this customer retention strategy

   B. by providing the medical sector with more accurate guidelines on patient retention and marketing

   C. by identifying the major factors underlying customer turnover rate

Situation 5

1. Why do governmental policymakers of social welfare trends and commercial investors rely strongly on forecasts?

   A. to identify factors that affect the elderly population

   B. to remain abreast of regulations that govern health finance policies and to develop new inventory project

   C. support a feasible health care policy strategy to meet the demand of this rapidly growing sector

2. Why must Taiwan effectively address the increasing demand for long-term healthcare facilities and services?

   A. because healthcare providers cannot resist expanding into this area

   B. because of its increasingly elderly population

   C. because forecasting (both supply and demand) trends in the long-term care market is a fundamental part of feasibility analysis

3. What have seldom been adopted to forecast trends in the long-term care market in Taiwan?

   A. expert conjectures

   B. previous sector growth factors

   C. modeling methods

4. How are critical factors associated with further development of Taiwan's long-term healthcare sector identified?

   A. from the questionnaire replies with reference to pertinent research

   B. from the elderly population in Taiwan

   C. from institutional managers, private sector investors and academics

5. Why is a GM (1, 1) model based on the Grey Theory is then developed?

   A. to forecast accurately the supply of Taiwan's long term care facilities and services

   B. to support a feasible health care policy strategy

C. to use data obtained from the Ministry of Interior's website

Situation 6

1. Why is the credit rating status of most Taiwanese enterprises often unknown?

   A. further exacerbation of the NPL crisis

   B. They are small- and medium-sized.

   C. a shortage of operating funds in banks

2. Why have banks expended considerable time and human resources in diagnosing the ability of enterprises to repay loans

   A. to determine current status and credit classification

   B. to loan to, or invest in, organizations based on whether they have a good credit rating

   C. to reduce non-performing loans

3. What will ultimately harm investor interests, stockholder profits and institutional reputations?

   A. lending and investing as common business practices of financial organizations

   B. further exacerbation of the NPL crisis that would cause a shortage of operating funds in banks

   C. investigations made by financial experts into financial reports to determine current status and credit classification

4. What causes misclassifications that result in inestimable losses?

   A. the inability of loaning institutions to estimate accurately the credit rating of enterprises

   B. the inability to increase the accuracy of expert systems owing to the inability to accurately predict credit ratings

   C. time-consuming and prohibitively expensive investigations that do not always yield satisfactory results

5. Why can't machine learning methods increase the accuracy of expert systems?

   A. owing to the inability to increase the efficiency of obtaining data from small-
and medium-sized enterprises

   B. owing to the inability to accurately predict credit ratings

   C. owing to the inability to reduce operational costs during estimation

O Reading Comprehension II
Select the word or expression whose meaning is closest
to the meaning of the underlined word or expression in
the following passages.

Situation 4

1. Neural networks are used to enhance the model <u>accuracy</u>, and the results are subsequently analyzed.

   A. veracity

   B. solecism

   C. erratum

2. In addition to providing the medical sector with more accurate guidelines on patient retention and marketing, the proposed model greatly helps hospitals to provide <u>high-quality</u> and flexible health care services that will ultimately enhance their public image by markedly improving relations with patients.

   A. inferior

   B. subordinate

   C. predominant

3. Apart from identifying the major factors underlying customer turnover rate, the proposed model can also offer <u>feasible</u> strategies to cope with this dilemma and achieve management goals.

   A. viable

   B. impervious

   C. preposterous

4. Furthermore, the proposed model can contribute to efforts to maintain customers in the highly competitive medical market sector and provide a <u>valuable</u> reference for healthcare managers in enhancing customer relations.

   A. nugatory

B. abject

C. esteemed

5. We seek your <u>approval</u> to adopt this customer retention strategy that can ultimately reduce the operating costs of hospitals and increase the total number of patients.

A. reproof

B. the nod

C. black ball

Situation 5

1. Following the submission of a questionnaire to institutional managers as well as public and private sector investors, critical factors associated with further development of Taiwan's long-term healthcare sector are identified from the replies with reference to <u>pertinent</u> research.

A. on target

B. extraneous

C. not germane

2. A GM (1, 1) model based on the Grey Theory is then developed to forecast accurately the supply of Taiwan's <u>long term</u> care facilities and services using data obtained from the Ministry of Interior's website.

A. ephemeral

B. fugacious

C. perennial

3. In addition to identifying factors that affect the elderly population, the <u>proposed</u> forecasting models measure precisely the demand for and supply of long-term healthcare resources in Taiwan.

A. contemplated

B. reneged

C. vitiated

4. Moreover, the proposed models not only are a valuable resource for institutional managers, private sector investors and academics, but also <u>support</u> a feasible health care policy strategy to meet the demand of this rapidly growing sector.

   A. leave stranded

   B. abandon

   C. buttress

5. We strongly recommend that your healthcare organization adopt these forecasting methods not only to determine the accuracy of forecasting reports, but also to determine what policies or <u>inventory</u> projects to implement.

   A. dissipated

   B. stockpile

   C. doled out

Situation 6

1. Additionally, the accuracy of the ANN classification machine is estimated with ten-fold cross <u>validation</u> to identify the most efficient machine.

   A. substantiation

   B. renunciation

   C. cold shoulder

2. Moreover, results obtained from the above tests are tabulated and compared with those in the literature to verify data <u>authenticity</u>.

   A. verity

   B. fabrication

   C. hogwash

3. The proposed classification model increases predictive accuracy from 10% (as achieved by the conventional classification system) to 80%, subsequently

reducing operating costs significantly.

A. dormant

B. modus operandi

C. abeyant

4. In addition to increasing the efficiency of obtaining data from small- and medium-sized enterprises, and reducing operational costs during estimation, the proposed model provides important <u>guidelines</u> for banks.

A. miscalculation

B. misinformation

C. specs

5. We therefore highly <u>recommend</u> that your institution adopt this novel classification model to increase your accuracy in classifying the credit ratings of lending enterprises and significantly lower administrative expenses.

A. remonstrate

B. extol

C. demur

Unit Four

Informal Technical Reports
非正式實用工程技術報告

- Identify the managerial motivations to undertake this project
  簡要地描述管理方案所關心的事項

- Briefly introduce the industrial setting in terms of customer concerns and the project group's priorities
  闡明特定部門或客戶所關心的工業環境

- Introduce the problem to be solved
  介紹管理問題

- Summarize the project goals
  介紹管理方案的目標

- Highlight the project methodology
  管理方案方法論的細節描述

- Summarize the main results of the project
  管理方案主要成果總結

- Describe how the project results contribute to a professional or academic field
  管理方案對特定部門或領域的全面貢獻

Vocabulary and related expressions

relax restrictions on	對……的限制鬆綁
over-the-counter drugs	非處方箋開立的藥劑
hierarchical levels	階層式層級
major success factors	成功的主因
one-stop shopping	一次購足
consumer purchasing factors	消費者購買因素
customer turnover rate	客戶周轉率
differentiating between	在……之間呈現差異化
confirm the reliability of	肯定……的信賴度
precautionary measures	預防措施
achieving management goals	達成管理目標
highly competitive medical market sector	高度（極度）競爭的醫療市場產業
the supply of and demand for	……的供應以及……的需求
significant public concern	民眾最關切的議題……
various operating costs	各式各樣的營運成本費用
customer satisfaction indexes	客戶（顧客）滿意度指數
digitize the data	將資料加以數位化
corporate management	公司管理
increasing popularity of	提高……受歡迎的程度
extensive customer data	大量的顧客數據資料
optimize marketing management practices	將行銷管理作法最佳化
diverse promotional strategies	多樣化的促銷策略
reducing promotional costs	降低促銷成本
ability to attract new customers	吸引新客戶的才能
implement marketing practices	實施行銷慣例
increase one's competitiveness	提高某人的競爭力
increasing medical costs and premiums	提高醫療成本和保險費
identifying and satisfying the needs of a patient	辨別、滿足患者的需求
significantly reducing overhead	大大（大規模）減少管銷費用
optimization procedure	最佳化程序（流程）
select the optimal location and size	嚴選最佳位置與大小
minimize societal risks	減小社會風險
stagnant economy	停滯不前的經濟態勢（情勢）
correctional facilities	懲治所
exhaustive literature review	徹底的回顧文獻
consultation with experts in the field	請教業界的專家

Situation 1

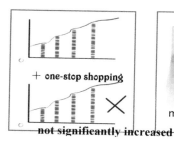

Situation 2

Situation 3

A Write down the key points of the situations on the preceding page, while the instructor reads aloud the script from the Answer Key. Alternatively, students can listen online at www.chineseowl.idv.tw.

Situation 1

_____

_____

_____

Situation 2

_____

_____

_____

Situation 3

_____

_____

_____

B Oral practice I

Based on the three situations in this unit, write three questions beginning with **Why**, and answer them. The questions do not need to come directly from these situations.

Examples

Why are consumers able to purchase over-the-counter drugs, vitamins and other medicines in supermarkets or through mass merchandisers?

because the Taiwanese government has relaxed restrictions on the domestic medical sector in recent years

Why did our project address how to identify major success factors of the pharmaceutical sector in Taiwan?

for purposes of devising more effective customer-based strategies

1._____

_____

2._____

_____

3._____

_____

C Based on the three situations in this unit, write three questions beginning with **What**, and answer them. The questions do not need to come directly from these situations.

Examples

What have hospitals heavily prioritized?

attracting new patients

What factors have led to the implementation of a Global Budget System?

the extremely competitive medical market sector in Taiwan and budget deficits associated with the island's National Health Insurance scheme

1.＿＿＿＿＿＿＿＿＿＿＿＿＿＿＿＿＿＿＿＿＿＿＿＿＿

＿＿＿＿＿＿＿＿＿＿＿＿＿＿＿＿＿＿＿＿＿＿＿＿＿

2.＿＿＿＿＿＿＿＿＿＿＿＿＿＿＿＿＿＿＿＿＿＿＿＿＿

＿＿＿＿＿＿＿＿＿＿＿＿＿＿＿＿＿＿＿＿＿＿＿＿＿

3.＿＿＿＿＿＿＿＿＿＿＿＿＿＿＿＿＿＿＿＿＿＿＿＿＿

＿＿＿＿＿＿＿＿＿＿＿＿＿＿＿＿＿＿＿＿＿＿＿＿＿

D Based on the three situations in this unit, write three questions beginning with **How**, and answer them. The questions do not need to come directly from these situations.

Examples

How has our group researched long-term healthcare in Taiwan?

by thoroughly exploring the difficulty of forecasting its supply and demand

How has significant public concern arisen?

over the fact that the institutional health care sector obviously varies greatly island wide in the level and quality of services and facilities

1._____

_____

2._____

_____

3._____

_____

E Write questions that match the answers provided.

1._____

_____

by using the analytic hierarchical process

2._____

_____

to design and implement precautionary measures to reduce customer turnover rates

3._____

_____

Taiwan's growing elderly population

F Listening Comprehension I

Situation 1

1. Why did our project address how to identify major success factors of the pharmaceutical sector in Taiwan?

   A. to strengthen consumer demand through one-stop shopping

   B. to enable pharmaceutical managers to execute business operations more effectively

   C. to devise more effective customer-based strategies

2. Why have consumers been able to purchase over-the-counter drugs, vitamins and other medicines in supermarkets or through mass merchandisers?

   A. because pharmacies have strengthened consumer demand through one-stop shopping

   B. because the Taiwanese government has relaxed restrictions on the domestic medical sector in recent years

   C. owing to the ability to analyze and rank major consumer purchasing factors using the analytic hierarchical process

3. How was the questionnaire in this study devised?

   A. by allowing pharmaceutical managers to modify marketing strategies based on inconsistencies between consumer demand and the response to that demands

   B. based on consumer purchasing factors identified from pertinent literature

   C. by incorporating consumer purchasing factors on various hierarchical levels

4. How does the proposed KSF model enable pharmaceutical managers to execute business operations more effectively?

   A. by incorporating consumer purchasing factors on various hierarchical levels to enable local pharmacies in Taiwan to reform their marketing strategies

   B. by sending questionnaires to consumers and pharmaceutical managers

C. by allowing them to modify marketing strategies based on inconsistencies between consumer demand and the response to that demands

5. What was the outcome of consumer purchases of over-the-counter drugs, vitamins and other medicines in supermarkets or through mass merchandisers?

   A. The Taiwanese government relaxed restrictions on the domestic medical sector in recent years.

   B. The profits of local pharmacies were negatively affected.

   C. Investor confidence in local pharmacies increased.

Situation 2

1. How would one characterize the medical market sector in Taiwan?

   A. heavily prioritized

   B. having received increasing attention

   C. extremely competitive

2. What are large budget deficits in Taiwan associated with?

   A. the island's Global Budget System

   B. the island's National Health Insurance scheme

   C. the island's hospital administrators

3. What has received increasing attention among hospitals?

   A. the patient turnover rate

   B. attracting new patients

   C. ability of healthcare managers to enhance customer relations

4. Why was a database of pertinent hospital patient data utilized and data mining used?

   A. to determine how to retain customers

   B. to design and implement precautionary measures to reduce customer turnover rates

   C. to identify the factors associated with the customer turnover rate

5. Who does the proposed model provide a valuable reference for when attempting to enhance customer relations?

   A. hospital administrators

   B. healthcare managers

   C. pertinent literature

Situation 3

1. What has Taiwan's growing elderly population increased the demand for?

   A. significant public concern

   B. enhanced patient care

   C. institutional-based health care

2. What has caused significant public concern?

   A. The institutional health care sector obviously varies greatly island wide in the level and quality of services and facilities.

   B. the difficulty of forecasting the supply of and demand for long-term healthcare in Taiwan

   C. a focus on legislation, human resource management and approaches to enhancing patient care

3. What has seldom been addressed?

   A. concern over the correlation between quality of institutional care and working capital

   B. legislation, human resource management and approaches to enhancing patient care

   C. the effect of various operating costs on the quality of institutional healthcare

4. What was used to analyze exactly how the quality and operating costs of institutional healthcare correlate with each other?

   A. legislation, human resource management and approaches

   B. relevant non-digitized data

C. financial statements and customer satisfaction indexes

5. What can the results of this study enable institutional healthcare facility managers to do?

A. strengthen areas of corporate management

B. provide high-quality long-term healthcare

C. both A and B

G Reading Comprehension I
Select the word or expression whose meaning is closest to the meaning of the underlined word or expression in the following passages

Situation 1

1. A questionnaire based on consumer purchasing factors identified from <u>pertinent</u> literature was sent to consumers and pharmaceutical managers.

   A. inapplicable

   B. pointless

   C. ad rem

2. Major <u>consumer</u> purchasing factors were then analyzed and ranked using the analytic hierarchical process.

   A. merchandiser

   B. end user

   C. marketer

3. The proposed KSF model enables pharmaceutical managers to execute business operations more effectively by allowing them to modify marketing strategies based on <u>inconsistencies</u> between consumer demand and the response to that demands.

   A. aberrations

   B. the norm

   C. same old thing

4. The proposed KSF model enables pharmaceutical managers to <u>execute</u> business operations more effectively by allowing them to modify marketing strategies based on inconsistencies between consumer demand and the response to that demands.

   A. shirk

   B. abandon

   C. percolate

5. Importantly, the proposed model can be applied to other <u>retail</u> stores, enhancing

   their business operations.

   A. noncommercial

   B. bartering

   C. personal

Situation 2

1. Pertinent literature was then reviewed to confirm the <u>reliability</u> of variables in

   the database.

   A. solidness

   B. questionability

   C. implausibility

2. Next, questionnaires were sent to hospital administrators regarding customer

   satisfaction, and the results were <u>subsequently</u> analyzed.

   A. previously

   B. latterly

   C. precedented

3. The proposed predictive model can be adopted to design and implement

   <u>precautionary</u> measures to reduce customer turnover rates.

   A. reconsideration

   B. afterthought

   C. inductive

4. In addition to identifying the major factors that <u>govern</u> customer turnover rate,

   the proposed model offers feasible strategies for overcoming this issue and

   achieving management goals.

   A. steer

B. supersede

C. supplant

5. Moreover, the proposed model contributes to efforts to maintain customers in the highly competitive medical market sector and provides a <u>valuable</u> reference for healthcare managers in enhancing customer relations.

A. cherished

B. abject

C. contemptible

Situation 3

1. Exactly how the quality and operating costs of institutional healthcare correlate with each other was analyzed using financial statements and customer <u>satisfaction</u> indexes.

A. dismay

B. satiety

C. chagrin

2. Relevant non-digitized data was then calculated using a gray system-based <u>mathematical</u> method and fuzzy theory.

A. literary

B. analytical

C. humanistic

3. After the fuzzy <u>theory</u> had been applied to digitize the data, the gray system was used to rank and verify the importance of various operating costs and the quality of institutional healthcare.

A. proof

B. reality

C. surmise

4. The results of this study <u>enable</u> institutional healthcare facility managers not

only to strengthen areas of corporate management, but also to provide high-quality long-term healthcare.

A. endow

B. inhibit

C. hinder

5. The results of this study enable institutional healthcare facility managers not only to strengthen areas of corporate management, but also to provide <u>high-quality</u> long-term healthcare.

A. exemplary

B. shoddy

C. pretentious

H Common elements in writing an informal technical report 非正式實用工程技術報告include the following elements:

a. 簡要地描述管理方案所關心的事項。經由一個句子描述管理機構對影響目標工業或客戶有關事項的關心程度。

範例 i

Our working group has become increasingly intrigued with how to devise appropriate strategies and procedures for implementing customer services based on available client data.

範例 ii

Educators expressed concern over how to increase the effectiveness of genetic algorithm (GA) courses.

b. 闡明特定部門或客戶所關心的工業環境：管理問題形成的工業環境背景描述。

範例 i

As a governmental subsidized, non-profit research organization, Industrial Technology Research Institute (ITRI) has established a hotline to handle customer concerns in a manner more fully consistent with the concept of being "customer-oriented". Via a unique phone line in the call center at ITRI, customers can query or request various services, as well as express their dissatisfaction with service quality. In response, ITRI provides an procedure for processing these calls. The hotline currently receives an average of 150-200 calls monthly, with a total of 4016 calls made domestically up to August 23, 2004. The call center generally focuses on integrating IT and communication technologies using a database that records all information on customer interactions.

範例 ii

An increasing number of GA courses are offered to solve optimization problems. As is well known, GAs seek optimum solutions in a desired search space. Many GA-related workshops and conferences have been held over the past three decades, owing to their diverse industrial applications. Such courses instill in students the essential role of experimental design and simulation in learning GAs.

c. 介紹管理問題：管理問題的本質和對與其相關的特定部門或客戶的負面影響。

範例 i

However, customer value is seldom analyzed nor is the performance of the service strategies evaluated.

範例 ii

However, students spend much time in coding programs for exercises when learning GAs, making it impossible for them to implement many GAs in a short time. Providing students with the opportunity to simulate GAs is essential in such a course. At the introductory level, teaching a new algorithm as an exercise is also expensive in terms of staff time, and can even be counterproductive since the student's written programs can introduce new problems. For instance, students who can implement only one GA in two weeks will learn GAs less effectively than those who can implement several. Moreover, students cannot implement all the concepts introduced in a GA course, owing to time and course load constraints.

d. 介紹管理方案的目標：管理機構對以上問題最合理的回應。

範例 i

Therefore, we examined previously unrecognized customer behavioral patterns.

Based on the results, we further recommended appropriate strategies and procedures for implementing customer services.

範例 ii

Therefore, we developed a novel learning environment, capable of assisting students in flexibly learning genetic algorithms based on computer-assisted instruction.

e. 管理方案方法論的細節描述：精確的方案步驟描述。

範例 i

Data were initially retrieved from the customer service system and then categorized. Areas of analysis were then assigned to research team members. Next, customer attributes and the category to which customer queries belong were determined. Finally, appropriate strategies and procedures for implementing customer services were recommended.

範例 ii

Several benchmark problems were integrated in this environment. A mathematical expression was then developed to provide users with fitness functions of GAs. Next, a case study involving a GA course was presented to demonstrate the effectiveness of the proposed environment.

f. 管理方案主要成果總結：管理方案對特定部門或客戶立即的利益。

範例 i

Combining qualitative and quantitative approaches, the content analysis approach not only converts qualitative data into quantitative data for statistical analysis, but also elucidates qualitative implications through an encoding process.

範例 ii

The proposed environment can reduce the time required for students to complete a GA assignment to one week, increasing the number of practice exercises that can be implemented and allowing them to better learn GAs. During simulation, the learning environment immediately informs the students of the current operational status so that they can interact with the computer. Moreover, a complete evolutionary process can be logged in files for further analysis.

g. 管理方案對特定部門或領域的全面貢獻：研究結果和所提方法對管理機構以外更廣大讀者的牽涉。

範例 i

Furthermore, the proposed method can analyze non-structural data efficiently.

範例 ii

Importantly, the novel learning environment can eliminate the need for hand coding GA programs, thus simplifying the process of learning genetic algorithms. While recognizing the critical role that simulation plays in learning GAs, the proposed learning environment facilitates operations so that many common problems can be addressed. Moreover, this environment enables students to select desired system configurations, including structural settings and parametric selections, before simulation.

In the space below, write an informal technical report.

_____

_____

_____

_____

_____

_____

_____

_____

_____

_____

Look at the following examples of an informal technical report.

範例 i

簡要地描述管理方案所關心的事項 Our working group has become increasing concerned over the growing incidence of failure in our company's digital receivers owing to carrier recovery problems. 闡明特定部門或客戶所關心的工業環境 Despite a large frequency offset, wide range locking with fast acquisition circuit-designed carrier recovery helps a digital receiver to lock the carrier frequency in a short time with a tolerable error rate. 介紹管理問題 However, conventional methods cannot do so just by utilizing digital a phase-locked loop (PLL) circuit since the loop filter is a one-order low-pass filter. For instance, while a loop filter with a wide bandwidth causes large vibration and ultimately a high error rate, a loop filter with a narrow bandwidth leads to slow convergence that takes over ten times longer than the estimated acquisition time. Furthermore, a loop filter with a narrow bandwidth may not recover the carrier while the receiver suffers from a large frequency or phase offset, leading to failure in the digital receiver. 介紹管理方案的目標 Therefore, we developed a numerical method to choose efficiently the bandwidth of the loop filter in the PLL circuit. An additional apparatus can also be developed in the carrier recovery circuit to estimate offsets precisely. 管理方案方法論的細節描述 A frequency detection apparatus was used in the carrier recovery circuit to lock the large frequency offset. The PLL circuit was then automatically switch the coefficients of the loop filter into distinct bandwidths to reduce vibration and to converge faster than conventional circuits. 管理方案主要成果總結 According to our results, the novel design can lock a wide range of offsets of more than 100 KHz in a short acquisition time with a symbol error rate of less than 0.01. 管理方案對特定部門或領域的全面貢獻 Importantly, the improved carrier recovery on a digital receiver can track better than conventional models, making telecommunication products more competitive.

範例 ii

簡要地描述管理方案所關心的事項 Product engineers recently expressed concern over difficulty in comparing manufacturing processes or selecting an alternative supplier of materials for production. 闡明特定部門或客戶所關心的工業環境 Engineers heavily emphasize applicability and accuracy when using a process capability index to evaluate how the performance of a process. 介紹管理問題 However, using conventional process capability indices to evaluate a non-normal distribution process often leads to inaccurate results. Additionally, calculating a point estimator with sampling data leads to inaccurately estimating the process capability index of the process population. Although sampling more data can increase the accuracy of an estimator, such an approach is costly and time consuming. The above limitations cause engineers to make errors when comparing manufacturing processes or selecting an alternative supplier. 介紹管理方案的目標 Therefore, we developed an appropriate process capability index based on Clement's and the Bootstrap methods to evaluate non-normal distribution processes. 管理方案方法論的細節描述 Clement's method was adopted to adjust the conventional indices. The bootstrap method was then applied to reduce the estimation error. Next, computer simulations evaluated different non-normal distribution processes to demonstrate the effectiveness of the proposed index. Additionally, a series of procedures was developed for engineers without a statistical background. 管理方案主要成果總結 As anticipated, the proposed index can effectively evaluate non-normal distribution processes. 管理方案對特定部門或領域的全面貢獻 Moreover, the proposed index and procedures can be easily adopted by engineers when comparing processes or selecting an alternative supplier.

Situation 4

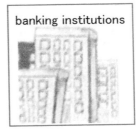

Situation 5

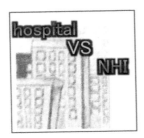

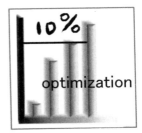

Situation 6

I Write down the key points of the situations on the preceding page, while the instructor reads aloud the script from the Answer Key. Alternatively, students can listen online at www.chineseowl.idv.tw.

Situation 4

_____

_____

_____

Situation 5

_____

_____

_____

Situation 6

_____

_____

_____

Oral practice II

Based on the three situations in this unit, write three questions beginning with *How*, and answer them. The questions do not need to come directly from these situations.

Examples

1. How does the bank's Board of Directors plan to identify, acquire and retain loyal and profitable customers?

   by more effectively managing customer relations

2. How have banking institutions been able to obtain extensive customer data?

   through the increasing popularity of card use and the growing number of Internet-based promotional activities in Taiwan

1.＿＿＿＿＿＿＿＿＿＿＿＿＿＿＿＿＿＿＿＿＿＿＿＿＿＿

＿＿＿＿＿＿＿＿＿＿＿＿＿＿＿＿＿＿＿＿＿＿＿＿＿＿

2.＿＿＿＿＿＿＿＿＿＿＿＿＿＿＿＿＿＿＿＿＿＿＿＿＿＿

＿＿＿＿＿＿＿＿＿＿＿＿＿＿＿＿＿＿＿＿＿＿＿＿＿＿

3.＿＿＿＿＿＿＿＿＿＿＿＿＿＿＿＿＿＿＿＿＿＿＿＿＿＿

＿＿＿＿＿＿＿＿＿＿＿＿＿＿＿＿＿＿＿＿＿＿＿＿＿＿

K Based on the three situations in this unit, write three questions beginning with **What**, and answer them. The questions do not need to come directly from these situations.

Examples

What is the purpose of the hospital's public relations department implementing marketing practices?

to increase our competitiveness in the medical sector

What are some of the concerns of governmental policy over Taiwan's National Health Insurance (NHI) scheme?

increasing medical costs and premiums as well as concern over the potential lowering of the quality of health care that is offered

1._____

_____

2._____

_____

3._____

_____

L Based on the three situations in this unit, write three questions beginning with **Why** and answer them. The questions do not need to come directly from these situations.

Examples

Why is selecting the optimal location and size of Taiwanese correctional facilities important?

to minimize societal risks

Why are the crime rates and subsequent convictions in Taiwan growing?

owing to the stagnant Taiwanese economy and increasing unemployment in recent years

1._____

_____

2._____

_____

3._____

_____

M Write questions that match the answers provided.

1._____

_____

by devising diverse promotional strategies or customizing products or services according to consumer needs

2._____

_____

by enabling them to develop an optimization procedure for marketing practices

3._____

_____

through an exhaustive literature review and consultation with experts in the field

N Listening Comprehension II

Situation 4

1. What factors explain continuous changes in governmental policy over Taiwan's National Health Insurance (NHI) scheme?

    A. a significant reduction of overhead and work time

    B. marketing practices that attract patients through public relations

    C. increasing medical costs and premiums as well as concern over the potential lowering of the quality of health care that is offered

2. How must hospitals emphasize marketing practices that attract patients?

    A. through public relations

    B. through marketing practices to increase competitiveness in the medical sector

    C. through increased competitiveness in the medical sector

3. By what percent can the proposed marketing strategy increase customer satisfaction?

    A. by over 5%

    B. by over 10%

    C. by over 20%

4. What has seldom been addressed?

    A. the role of public relations in business marketing

    B. the role of public relations in conducting personal interviews

    C. the role of public relations in hospital marketing

5. How can the proposed marketing strategy help hospital managers?

    A. to elucidate the role of public relations in business marketing

    B. to develop an optimization procedure for marketing practices

    C. to identify and satisfy the needs of a patient

Situation 5

1. Why does a hospital's public relations department want to implement marketing practices?

    A. to lower medical costs

    B. to increase our competitiveness in the medical sector

    C. to significantly reduce overhead and work time

2. Why does governmental policy over Taiwan's National Health Insurance (NHI) scheme continuously change?

    A. because of increasing medical costs and premiums

    B. because of concern over the potential lowering of the quality of health care that is offered

    C. both A and B

3. How must hospitals emphasize marketing practices that attract patients?

    A. by identifying and satisfying the needs of a patient

    B. develop an optimization procedure for marketing practices

    C. through public relations

4. What has seldom been addressed?

    A. the role of public relations in business marketing

    B. the role of public relations in hospital marketing

    C. the role of public relations in the National Health Insurance system

5. How was factor analysis of a customer's needs performed?

    A. by conducting personal interviews

    B. by identifying vital factors

    C. by significantly reducing overhead and work time

Situation 6

1. How can one minimize societal risks?

    A. by selecting the optimal location and size of Taiwanese correctional facilities

B. by enabling correctional facilities to operate under a governmental budget

C. by alleviating the concerns of residents near a newly established correctional facility

2. What factors have led to a high prisoner population?

A. the subjective judgment of decision makers and the security of an inmate population

B. the optimal target population and location of future correctional facilities

C. growing crime rates and subsequent convictions

3. What does the conventional means of selecting the locations of correctional facilities often depend on?

A. the stagnant Taiwanese economy and increasing unemployment in recent years

B. the subjective judgment of decision makers

C. the optimal target population and location of future correctional facilities

4. Why are factors that affect the infrastructure and safety of correctional facilities in Taiwan identified?

A. by using the analytic hierarchy process (AHP) to determine the optimal target population and location of such facilities

B. by reducing the cost of facility operations and maintenance-related management

C. by encouraging other law enforcement organizations to understand how location planning can ensure the security of an inmate population

5. How were location-related factors identified?

A. by using AHP

B. through an exhaustive literature review and consultation with experts in the field

C. based on the analysis results

O Reading Comprehension II
Select the word or expression whose meaning is closest to the meaning of the underlined word or expression in the following passages.

Situation 4

1. Those behavioral results are used to devise diverse promotional strategies or <u>customize</u> products or services according to consumer needs, thus achieving market differentiation and effective management of customer relations.

   A. homogenize

   B. standardize

   C. mutate

2. Using the proposed model, factors of the ranking module are <u>verified</u> and adjusted to ensure that a company continuously provides quality services.

   A. discredited

   B. documented

   C. disparaged

3. The proposed customer ranking model can be adopted to manage effectively customer relations, significantly reducing promotional costs and allowing sales staff to <u>concentrate</u> on identifying potential customers.

   A. pay no attention

   B. let one's mind wander

   C. ruminate

4. The customer's value can be determined and this model significantly enhances the <u>ability</u> to attract new customers.

   A. dexterity

   B. enervation

   C. malady

5. Furthermore, it can be used in other business sectors to enhance the ability to identify, acquire and retain <u>loyal</u> and profitable customers.

A. frigid

B. apathetic

C. vehement

Situation 5

1. Therefore, we <u>launched</u> a marketing strategy for our hospital that emphasizes identifying and satisfying the needs of a patient.

A. sequestered

B. propelled

C. eluded

2. Factor analysis of a customer's needs was performed by conducting <u>personal</u> interviews.

A. conjoint

B. privy

C. conjunct

3. The results were then analyzed, and <u>vital</u> factors identified.

A. superficial

B. skin-deep

C. meat-and-potatoes

4. The proposed marketing strategy increases customer satisfaction by over 10% through hospital marketing, by significantly reducing <u>overhead</u> and work time.

A. outlay

B. nest egg

C. kitty

5. The proposed marketing strategy provides a valuable <u>reference</u> for hospital managers to develop an optimization procedure for marketing practices.

A. abjuration

B. abnegation

C. source book

Situation 6

1. The optimal target population and location of <u>future</u> correctional facilities are determined from the analysis results.

   A. impending

   B. precedent

   C. extinct

2. The concerns of residents near a newly established correctional facility can be <u>alleviated</u> by reassuring them of the security features and pointing out the potential economic benefits of the facility.

   A. exacerbated

   B. aggravated

   C. pacified

3. While correctional facilities operate under a governmental budget, the optimal location can reduce the cost of facility operations and <u>maintenance</u>-related management.

   A. liquidation

   B. devastation

   C. prolongation

4. The results of this study provide a valuable reference for governmental authorities in selecting the optimal location and size of correctional facilities, <u>minimizing</u> societal risk.

   A. curtailing

   B. aerating

   C. pyramiding

5. Furthermore, this optimal location strategy <u>encourages</u> other law enforcement organizations to understand how location planning can ensure the security of an inmate population, reduce societal risks and alleviate public concern by making local residents aware of the potential benefits of such facilities.

A. appalls

B. emboldens

C. vexes

Unit Five

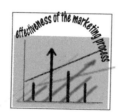

Employment Application Letters

求職申請信函

· Apply for a specific job by referring to an advertisement, mutual friend or other source of information about a particular line of work
經由廣告、朋友及其他相關訊息得知的工作申請

· Summarize ones' academic and professional qualifications in relation to the needs of your potential employer
對未來工作的個人學術及相關專業特質總結

· Compliment the organization that you are applying to and state how work there would benefit one's career goals
讚揚要申請工作的機構及說明其對個人工作目標所產生的利益

· Sum up the memo with one main theme or selling point
總結主要論點

· Invite the reader to contact you for an interview
邀請讀者給予面試機會

Vocabulary and related expressions

departmental curriculum	部門籌辦的課程
sparked one's interest in	激發某人的興趣
focus one's graduate study on	某人的畢業論文主題焦點在於
facilitate patient recovery	有助於患者（病人）的恢復（復原）
comprehensive and challenging training	包羅萬象、極具挑戰性的訓練（課程）
optimum dosage level	最適合的劑量
matches one's career direction	符合某人的事業方向
commercial development planning	商業發展規劃（計畫）
resolve problems efficiently	有效地解決問題
unforeseeable problems	無法預測的問題
diverse range	各式各樣的範圍
logistics management	物流管理
information technology sector	資訊科技部門
practical work setting	實際工作環境
further refine one's skills	進一步改善某人的技巧
logical competence and analytical skills	邏輯能力和分析技巧
intensive graduate level training	密集進行研究生一級的培訓
corporate family	企業家族
solid experience and management skills	紮實的經驗與管理技巧
dynamics of one's profession	某人的職業動態
remain abreast of	與……並駕齊驅
satisfy consumer demands	滿足消費者需求
integrate one's management experiences with theoretical knowledge	
	整合某人管理經驗與理論知識
elevate the quality of	提升……的品質
extracurricular activities	課外活動
become oriented with one's new responsibilities	以擔負某人全新責任為主要目的
securing employment	確保就業
equip one with the necessary skills	讓某人具備必要技巧
diverse academic interests	各種學術利益
see beyond the conventional limits of a discipline	洞悉紀律隱含的古老束縛
competent candidate	足以勝任的候選人
constantly fluctuating customer requirements	顧客（客戶）要求不斷變動
explore beyond the surface of	探索……表象的背後
conceptualize problems in different ways	以不同方式將問題概念化
broaden one's perspective of	放大某人的……觀點
business transactions models	業務交易模式

Situation 1

Mary Li

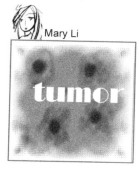

therapeutic treatment

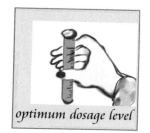

optimum dosage level

Situation 2

John Chuang

Commercial development planning

offering famous medical product brands

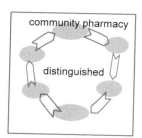

community pharmacy

distinguished

Situation 3

Julie Yeh

advertised

corporate family

outstanding product research and technical capabilities

A Write down the key points of the situations on the preceding page, while the instructor reads aloud the script from the Answer Key. Alternatively, students can listen online at www.chineseowl.idv.tw.

Situation 1

_____

_____

_____

Situation 2

_____

_____

_____

Situation 3

_____

_____

_____

B Oral practice I

Based on the three situations in this unit, write three questions beginning with **Why**, and answer them. The questions do not need to come directly from these situations.

Examples

Why does Mary feel highly qualified for the advertised research position of a radiotechnologist?

because of her strong academic background and practical experiences

Why did the departmental curriculum at National Taipei University sparked Mary's interest in various directions?

because she subsequently developed an interest in medical imagery and radiotherapy of tumors, particularly for curative purposes

1._____

_____

2._____

_____

3._____

_____

C Based on the three situations in this unit, write three questions beginning with **What**, and answer them. The questions do not need to come directly from these situations.

Examples

What closely matches John's career direction and previous academic training?

the position of a pharmaceutical sales representative recently advertised in the February 5, 2007 edition of The China Times

What has enthralled John since he took part in a business management training course sponsored by the Council of Labor Affairs?

commercial development planning

1._____

_____

2._____

_____

3._____

_____

D Based on the three situations in this unit, write three questions beginning with **Where**, and answer them. The questions do not need to come directly from these situations.

Examples

Where was the marketing position in the information technology sector advertised recently?

in the March issue of Information Today

Where did Julie acquire many valuable research experiences through graduate studies in Business Management?

at National Taiwan Ocean University

1._____

_____

2._____

_____

3._____

_____

E   Write questions that match the answers provided.

1. _____

   _____

   September

2. _____

   _____

   while pursuing a graduate degree

3. _____

   _____

   during two years of intensive graduate level training

F Listening Comprehension I

Situation 1

1. In what month's edition of Hospital Administrator Magazine did Mary see the advertisement for the research position of a radiotechnologist?

   A. June

   B. December

   C. September

2. What sparked Mary's interest in various directions?

   A. the departmental curriculum at National Taipei University

   B. the departmental curriculum at National Taiwan University of Science and Technology

   C. the departmental curriculum at National Taipei University

3. What have several years of academic study deeply impressed with?

   A. the notion that radiation therapy of tumors can facilitate patient recovery

   B. the notion that study is not just for securing employment

   C. the notion that she can contribute to the overall welfare of those patients who are seeking therapeutic treatment

4. What reflects Mary's commitment to pursuing a research career?

   A. her recent completion of a Master's degree in Medical Imagery

   B. her interest in medical imagery and radiotherapy of tumors, particularly for curative purposes

   C. her contribution to the overall welfare of those patients who are seeking therapeutic treatment

5. What area of research has received increasing attention in recent years?

   A. how to estimate the optimum dosage level for tumor patients efficiently and accurately

   B. how radiation therapy of tumors can facilitate patient recovery

C. how to contribute to the overall welfare of those patients who are seeking therapeutic treatment

Situation 2

1. What closely matches John's career direction and previous academic training?

   A. commercial development planning

   B. the position of a pharmaceutical sales representative recently advertised in The China Times

   C. marketing research

2. What organization sponsored the business management training course that John enrolled in?

   A. the Council of Labor Affairs

   B. the Department of Healthcare Management

   C. Yuanpei University

3. When did John learn of advanced theories in his field and acquire practical training?

   A. while pursuing a graduate degree

   B. while overcoming operational difficulties and maintaining good discipline to manage its business units effectively

   C. while attempting to contribute to the development of management strategies in order to resolve unforeseeable problems efficiently

4. Why does John have the competence to contribute to the development of management strategies to resolve unforeseeable problems efficiently?

   A. because he has offered famous medical product brands from the United States in the Taiwan market

   B. because he has distinguished himself in overcoming operational difficulties and maintaining good discipline

   C. because he closely studied business practices in the medical sector

5. Why will John contact the company shortly by telephone?

    A. to see if the position is still available

    B. to provide further professional details

    C. to schedule an interview

Situation 3

1. How did Julie acquire many valuable research experiences?

    A. through her undergraduate studies in Business Management at National Taiwan Ocean University

    B. through her graduate studies in Business Management at National Taiwan University

    C. through her graduate studies in Business Management at National Taiwan Ocean University

2. When did Julie's logical competence and analytical skills reach new heights?

    A. during her two years of intensive graduate level training

    B. during her three years of intensive graduate level training

    C. during her two years of intensive undergraduate level training

3. What will definitely make Julie an asset to any collaborative product development effort?

    A. her ability to excel in information technology

    B. the particular expertise developed in graduate school and her strong academic and practical knowledge skills

    C. her ability to quickly absorb new information and adapt to new situations

4. What is Julie especially interested in?

    A. the company's state-of-the-art products and services, as well as outstanding product research and technical capabilities

    B. the role of information technology in devising marketing strategies for research purposes

C. how the company's marketing and related management departments reach strategic decisions

5. What has proved especially effective in devising marketing strategies for research purposes?

A. Julie's exposure to new fields

B. Julie's ability to excel in information technology

C. Julie's independent research capabilities and statistical as well as analytical skills

G Reading Comprehension I
Select the word or expression whose meaning is closest to the meaning of the underlined word or expression in the following passages.

Situation 1

1. Such training could provide me a <u>marvelous</u> opportunity to put my above knowledge and expertise into practice.

    A. run-of-the-mill

    B. prodigious

    C. quotidian

2. If employed at your hospital, I will apply my professional knowledge of how to estimate the optimum dosage level for tumor patients <u>efficiently</u> and accurately.

    A. prodigally

    B. ineptly

    C. facilely

3. My professional knowledge will <u>directly</u> facilitate the recovery of tumor patients undergoing therapy.

    A. verbatim

    B. obliquely

    C. slantingly

4. I am confident that my solid academic background in radiological technology will prove to be an <u>invaluable</u> asset to your hospital.

    A. indispensable

    B. trivial

    C. expendable

5. I look forward to meeting with you in person to discuss this position <u>further</u>.

    A. circumcised

B. subordinate

C. supplementary

Situation 2

1. Specifically, I hope to contribute to your marketing efforts, logistics management and medical research in areas that are <u>likely</u> to grow in the future.

   A. up-and-coming

   B. improbable

   C. dubious

2. As a community pharmacy chain, your franchiser has distinguished itself in overcoming operational difficulties and maintaining good <u>discipline</u> to manage its business units effectively.

   A. tumult

   B. pandemonium

   C. indoctrination

3. I firmly believe that if I successful in <u>securing</u> employment at your company, my strong academic and practical knowledge, curricular and otherwise, will enable me to contribute positively to your corporation.

   A. dissipating

   B. expending

   C. cinching

4. In summary, my marketing research and <u>excellent</u> analytical capabilities will support your company's commitment to offering quality products and services.

   A. tripe

   B. meritorious

   C. warped

5. I will contact you shortly by telephone with the <u>hope</u> of scheduling an interview.

A. utopia

B. dyspepsia

C. glumness

Situation 3

1. Employment at your company will undoubtedly <u>expose</u> me to new fields as long as I remain open and do not restrict myself to the range of my previous academic training.

   A. divulge

   B. enshroud

   C. burrow

2. In sum, my ability to <u>excel</u> in information technology proved especially effective in devising marketing strategies for research purposes.

   A. surmount (correct answer)

   B. blunder

   C. flounder

3. Despite lacking knowledge of a particular topic at the outset, I quickly <u>absorb</u> new information and adapt to new situations.

   A. dissipate

   B. fritter away

   C. imbibe

4. I believe that your company will find this a highly <u>desired</u> quality.

   A. felicitous

   B. gauche

   C. maladroit

5. Please contact me at your earliest <u>convenience</u> to schedule an interview.

   A. nuisance

   B. amenity

   C. exasperation

H Common elements in writing an employment application letter 撰寫求職申請信函的通則 include the following elements:

a. Apply for a specific job by referring to an advertisement, mutual friend, or other source of information about job. 藉由參考廣告、朋友互相交流或其他有關工作方面的資訊來源找一份特定的工作。

範例 i

I would like to apply for the position of marketing coordinator in the IAB-LP program that you advertised in the March issue of <u>Management Today</u>.

範例 ii

Please find enclosed my resume for employment as a business manager in your company, as advertised in the July edition of Corporate Finance.

b. Summarize one's academic and professional qualifications in relation to the needs of your potential employer. 因應未來雇主的潛在需求，簡短摘述某人的學經歷背景與相關資格。

範例 i

My fascination with strategic planning can be traced back to my senior year in the Department of Finance at National Dong Hwa University when I coordinated a seminar for the private sector. Marketing of consumer goods is a highly intriguing topic for me because such goods are closely related to daily life, and financial planners must devise various strategies to sell products in the face of rapidly changing consumer preferences.

範例 ii

While majoring in Management Science with a minor in Computer Science from

National Chiao Tung University, I spent considerable time developing an interest in technology applications such as the Internet and online databases. Given the numerous opportunities in this rapidly emerging sector, I received much academic and practical training from courses that equipped me with analytical skills and strong fundamentals in information technology.

c. Compliment the organization that you are applying to and state how work there would benefit one's career goals. 稱讚你正在應徵的企業組織，並說明該職位可能如何有助於達成某人的事業目標。

範例 i

Following its establishment in 1992, your organization distinguished itself as the first of its kind in Taiwan. Since its inception, your organizational scope has widened with extensive information management capabilities while adopting a multi-disciplinary approach.

範例 ii

While attracted to your company's diligent efforts in providing comprehensive financial services, I look forward to the opportunity to work in your company, enabling me to fully realize my career aspirations in the banking sector.

d. Sum up the memo with a main theme or selling point. 將主題或賣點在便條紙上總結

範例 i

Working in your corporation would be a life transforming experience. Given such an opportunity, I will integrate my theoretical training, previous experiences and creativity, as well as aggressively pursue future opportunities and strive to achieve corporate missions.

範例 ii

Joining the ABC corporate family would be a life changing experience. I will combine my education, previous experiences and enthusiasm to rise to the challenges of your intensely competitive working environment. I am also confident in my ability to perform tasks efficiently, as well as adjust to your company's organizational culture.

e. Invite the reader to contact you for an interview. 敬邀讀者與您連絡面試方面的事宜。

範例 i

I look forward to the opportunity to work in your company, enabling me to fully realize my career aspirations. Thank you in advance for your careful consideration.

範例 ii

I anxiously look forward to your favorable response.

In the space below, write an employment application letter.

_____

_____

_____

_____

_____

_____

_____

_____

_____

_____

Employment Application Letters
求職申請信函

Look at the following examples of an employment application letter.

範例 i

Employment at your company would allow me to nurture my brainstorming skills in a production-intensive environment. I have chosen your company for employment because of its global reputation as an incubator of technological innovation. As a graduate student of Industrial Engineering at National Chiao Tung University, I constantly focused on acquiring analytical skills and knowledge that are necessary in the workplace. In addition to completing the core curricular requirements, I took courses such as Finance and Supply Chains to understand more about commercial operations. Professors within the department provided especially valuable instruction on IC manufacturing management. The research process not only clarified concepts taught in class, but also allowed me to attain advanced professional knowledge by operating relevant software and interviewing upper-level management of real enterprises. Such practical experience will facilitate my transition from university life to the workplace. Moreover, in my master's thesis, I not only learned the method of writing a research paper, but also strengthened my ability to design a study, evaluate data, and orally communicate result. In addition to my diligence towards course work (as evidenced by my solid academic record), I participated in several extracurricular activities and took part-time jobs to ensure the necessary balance between academic and social skills. Through such activities, I broadened my perspective of how to handle routine tasks systematically and efficiently. Moreover, my calm nature and objective frame of mind allows me to communicate with others when preparing, planning, and coordinating numerous activities. In sum, my personal traits such as gregariousness, seriousness, responsible nature, humility, enthusiasm, and perseverance are conducive to your company's working environment. Reflecting upon my academic career up until now, I am anxious to understand how much this knowledge will provide a blueprint for my career. Continually learning and absorbing new information appear to be the only means of remaining abreast of the latest trends and renewing one's core value. Despite the volatility of financial markets and the uncertainty of economic circumstances, I look forward to the future. I am also confident of my ability to perform tasks efficiently, and to adjust to your company's organizational culture. Moreover, as a member of your corporation, I would wholeheartedly contribute to your company's goals. I look forward to arranging an interview with you at your earliest convenience to see how my above expertise can meet your organizational needs.

Situation 4

Sally Huang

hospital is recruiting

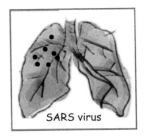

SARS virus

Situation 5

Jason Tong

decisions efficiently

efficiently

strong analytical and problem-solving skills

Situation 6

Scott Liao

semiconductor industry

UNIX-based systems

e-business

I Write down the key points of the situations on the preceding page, while the instructor reads aloud the script from the Answer Key. Alternatively, students can listen online at www.chineseowl.idv.tw.

Situation 4

_____

_____

_____

Situation 5

_____

_____

_____

Situation 6

_____

_____

_____

J Oral practice II
Based on the three situations in this unit, write three questions beginning with **How**, and answer them. The questions do not need to come directly from these situations.

Examples

How did Sally learn that the hospital is recruiting for a supervisor in the emergency care department?

from a recent March 15th posting on the *Nursing Today* website

How has Sally been involved in many efforts that require critical patient care?

by responding to the devastating Chi Chi earthquake that hit Taiwan on September 21, 2000, setting up a medical station at San Xia Da Bao River, and counteracting the deadly SARS virus in our hospital environment

1._____

_____

2._____

_____

3._____

_____

K Based on the three situations in this unit, write three questions beginning with **What**, and answer them. The questions do not need to come directly from these situations.

Examples

What will definitely help Jason become oriented with his new responsibilities at the company?

abundant experience of administrative work while in the military, and extracurricular activities in the student association at university

What is another strong asset that Jason brings to the company?

his familiarity with several analytic methods in decision science

1._____

_____

2._____

_____

3._____

_____

L Based on the three situations in this unit, write three questions beginning with **Why** and answer them. The questions do not need to come directly from these situations.

Examples

Why will Scott be able to satisfy constantly fluctuating customer requirements in information integration projects?

because of his love of challenges

Why has Scott been able to deal carefully with others and resolve disputes efficiently?

because of his project management experience

1._____

_____

2._____

_____

3._____

_____

M Write questions that match the answers provided.

1._____

_____

from her early nursing experience to her current work as a professional nurse in
an emergency care department

2._____

_____

in the high quality services that it provides to its customers

3._____

_____

critical thinking skills developed during undergraduate and graduate training

N Listening Comprehension II

Situation 4

1. In what department is the hospital recruiting for a supervisor?

   A. emergency medical network

   B. emergency care

   C. Business Management

2. What makes Sally confident of her ability to handle required administrative tasks?

   A. her decade of experience in emergency care departments and graduate degree in Business Management

   B. her solid nursing experience and management skills

   C. her ability to train emergency care professionals and assess the process and preparation of emergency medical staff

3. What does Sally remain fascinated by?

   A. the dynamics of her profession

   B. efforts to elevate the quality of healthcare management

   C. efforts to satisfy the demands of medical consumers while effectively controlling overhead

4. What makes Sally more adept in making the correct strategic decisions in the hospital's emergency medical unit?

   A. the ability to significantly contribute to efforts to train emergency care professionals and assess the process and preparation of emergency medical staff

   B. the ability to train emergency care professionals and assess the process and preparation of emergency medical staff

   C. the ability to integrate her substantial management experiences with theoretical knowledge

5. Where will the hospital establish a second medical center in the near future?

  A. in Taipei County

  B. in Taipei City

  C. in Taipei prefecture

Situation 5

1. What will definitely help Jason become oriented with his new responsibilities at the company?

  A. his knowledge of modern business practices and English writing skills to publish my research findings

  B. his diverse academic interests and strong curricular training

  C. abundant experience of administrative work while in the military, and extracurricular activities in the student association at university

2. What is another strong asset that Jason brings to the company?

  A. his familiarity with several analytic methods in decision science

  B. his strong communicative, organizational and management skills

  C. strong analytical and problem-solving skills

3. What will enable the organization to reach management decisions efficiently?

  A. Jason's ability to contribute significantly to the workplace

  B. Jason's ability to comprehend and familiarize himself with all of the commercial practices of the healthcare organization

  C. Jason's ability to explain results of analyses more clearly

4. In what field is the company a renowned leader?

  A. the finance sector

  B. the long-term healthcare sector

  C. the cosmetics sector

5. What type of organization is Jason applying to for employment?

  A. governmental

B. non-profit

C. hi-tech

Situation 6

1. What has Scott's project management experience enabled him to do?

    A. contribute more significantly to the organization's excellence in marketing

    B. deal carefully with others and resolve disputes efficiently

    C. upgrade e-business operations, such as online queries, payments and account transferals

2. How long has Scott devoted himself to developing information systems in the semiconductor industry?

    A. for nearly a decade

    B. for more than two decades

    C. for over a decade

3. How has Scott developed a particular interest in enhancing work productivity?

    A. by using the latest information technologies

    B. by effectively dealing with unforeseeable emergencies and enhancing customer services

    C. by addressing effectively information technology-related problems

4. For what purpose did Scott spend considerable time in researching system integration?

    A. for exploring beyond the surface of manufacturing-related issues and delving into their underlying implications

    B. for developing manufacturing applications on UNIX-based systems

    C. for conceptualizing problems in different ways

5. Why did Scott learn how to address supply chain-related issues?

    A. to broaden his perspective of potential applications of finance and decision making

B. to satisfy constantly fluctuating customer requirements in information integration projects

C. to upgrade e-business operations, such as online queries, payments and account transferals

O Reading Comprehension II
Select the word or expression whose meaning is closest
to the meaning of the underlined word or expression in
the following passages.

Situation 4

1. In addition to my background in the nursing profession, I strive constantly to
   <u>integrate</u> my substantial management experiences with theoretical knowledge,
   making me more adept in making the correct strategic decisions in our hospital'
   s emergency medical unit.

   A. conjoin

   B. dichotomize

   C. dissever

2. I am confident of my ability to contribute significantly to your efforts to <u>elevate</u>
   the quality of healthcare management if given the opportunity to work in your
   organization.

   A. emanate

   B. stilt

   C. precipitate

3. The <u>attached</u> resume includes my contact details.

   A. autarchic

   B. non-aligned

   C. imbued

4. Please give me this <u>opportunity</u>.

   A. fighting chance

   B. straits

   C. abjection

Situation 5

1. This strong organizational <u>commitment</u> is reflected in the high quality services that you provide to your customers.

   A. devoir

   B. refutation

   C. disproof

2. As a member of your corporation, I hope to participate actively in your company's <u>external</u> affairs.

   A. visceral

   B. indigenous

   C. peripheral

3. My work experience and solid academic background will enable me to comprehend and <u>familiarize</u> myself with all of the commercial practices of your healthcare organization in a relatively short time.

   A. discriminate

   B. orient

   C. differentiate

4. In addition to a solid academic background, a good manager should have strong <u>communicative</u>, organizational and management skills.

   A. introspective

   B. demure

   C. garrulous

5. I am confident that I possess them. I look forward to meeting with you in person to discuss in detail what this position <u>encompasses</u>.

   A. sidelines

   B. environs

   C. debars

Situation 6

1. Renowned for effectively dealing with unforeseeable <u>emergencies</u> and enhancing customer services, your company has established a vision that deeply impresses me.

   A. placidity

   B. repose

   C. predicaments

2. Moreover, I am attracted to your company's advanced financial information system for analyzing business transactions models, a system which will equip me with the competence to contribute more significantly to your organization's <u>excellence</u> in marketing.

   A. glitch

   B. arête

   C. blemish

3. If I am successful in gaining employment in your company, both my solid academic training and my research on information system development will make me a strong asset in your efforts to <u>upgrade</u> e-business operations, such as online queries, payments and account transferals.

   A. languish

   B. ebb

   C. boost

4. I am confident that my work experience in software development has equipped me with the <u>necessary</u> competence to address effectively information technology-related problems in your company.

   A. exigent

   B. exorbitant

   C. wanton

5. Please contact me at your earliest convenience to schedule an interview.

A. pigeonhole

B. pencil in

C. hang fire

Unit Six

John Li

Training Application Letters

訓練申請信函

- Request professional training
  科技訓練申請

- Summarize one's academic or professional experiences
  某人學歷及工作經驗概述

- Commend the organization to receive technical training from
  讚揚提供科技訓練的機構

- Explain the details of the technical training
  科技訓練細節解釋

Vocabulary and related expressions

self-supported guest researcher	自費的客座研究員
provide further details of	提供……進一步的詳細資料
a project aimed at	專案旨於……
effective prognostic method	有效的預後方法
adequate therapeutic treatment	適當的治療處理方式
elevate the curative rate	提升治癒率
management proficiency	管理效益
a wide array of theoretical concepts	種類繁多的理論概念
a long tradition of commitment	長期累積的承諾慣例
extensive training courses	廣泛的訓練課程
definitely benefit one's professional development	絕對有助於某人未來的專業發展
further one's knowledge skills	增進某人的知識運用技巧
strengthen one's expertise	加強某人的專業
compensate for one's lack of training	補償某人缺漏的訓練課程
improve one's expertise continually	持續改進某人的專業素養
clinical implications	臨床意義
contribute to one's ongoing efforts	奉獻一己之力，與某人共同投入
facilitate the diagnosis and treatment of	有助於對……的診斷和治療
dynamic work	動態工作
close collaboration among researchers	結束研究員之間的合作
underlying causes of	……的基本肇因
frequent publications in international journals	經常在國際期刊上發表作品
strict adherence to	嚴守……
proficient in the use of	精通……的使用
opportunity to serve in	有機會在……服務
highly adept investigator	技巧相當純熟的調查員
apply theoretical concepts in a practical context	在實務上運用理論概念
impressive training courses	讓人印象深刻的訓練課程
details of this proposed researcher position	有關這份推薦的研究員職位的詳細資料
rising cancer death rate	上升的罹患癌症死亡率
gain further exposure to	進一步獲得在……曝光
nurture one's talent	栽培某人的天分
widen one's range of interests	擴大某人的利益範疇
grasp fully the latest concepts	全面掌握最新概念
absorb tremendous amounts of information	吸收大量資訊
combine commercial success with innovation	在商業改革過程中獲得勝利
practicum internship	實習輔導

Situation 1

John Li

Situation 2

Mary Chang

Situation 3

Lisa Yeh

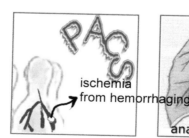
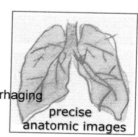

A Write down the key points of the situations on the preceding page, while the instructor reads aloud the script from the Answer Key. Alternatively, students can listen online at www.chineseowl.idv.tw.

Situation 1

_____

_____

_____

Situation 2

_____

_____

_____

Situation 3

_____

_____

_____

B Oral practice I

Based on the three situations in this unit, write three questions beginning with **Why**, and answer them. The questions do not need to come directly from these situations.

Examples

Why would John like to serve as a self-supported guest researcher in the oncology department of a hospital?

to build upon his academic and professional experience

Why did John actively participate in a project aimed at identifying prognostic factors of breast cancer?

to develop an effective prognostic method in order to increase the survival rate of breast cancer patients

1._____

_____

2._____

_____

3._____

_____

C Based on the three situations in this unit, write three questions beginning with **What**, and answer them. The questions do not need to come directly from these situations.

Examples

What did Mary's academic advisor, Dr. Cheng, recommend her to do?

contact the laboratory regarding the possibility of a guest researcher stay

What is Mary's main reason for receiving further training at the hospital?

owing to its commitment to excellent medical image processing as well as advanced PACS instrumentation

1.＿＿＿＿＿＿＿＿＿＿＿＿＿＿＿＿＿＿＿＿＿＿＿＿＿＿＿＿

＿＿＿＿＿＿＿＿＿＿＿＿＿＿＿＿＿＿＿＿＿＿＿＿＿＿＿＿＿

2.＿＿＿＿＿＿＿＿＿＿＿＿＿＿＿＿＿＿＿＿＿＿＿＿＿＿＿＿

＿＿＿＿＿＿＿＿＿＿＿＿＿＿＿＿＿＿＿＿＿＿＿＿＿＿＿＿＿

3.＿＿＿＿＿＿＿＿＿＿＿＿＿＿＿＿＿＿＿＿＿＿＿＿＿＿＿＿

＿＿＿＿＿＿＿＿＿＿＿＿＿＿＿＿＿＿＿＿＿＿＿＿＿＿＿＿＿

D Based on the three situations in this unit, write three questions beginning with **How**, and answer them. The questions do not need to come directly from these situations.

Examples

How is Lisa eager to strengthen her expertise in the hospital's Medical Imagery Department?

by optimizing the results obtained from the picture archiving communication system

How does Lisa hope to compensate for her lack of training in using the picture archiving communication system?

by serving as a self-supported guest worker for six months

1._____

_____

2._____

_____

3._____

_____

E Write questions that match the answers provided.

1._____

_____

for a three-month period

2._____

_____

by providing an excellent research environment, advanced equipment and related resources

3._____

_____

how to integrate diagnostic programs with the Internet and related technologies

F Listening Comprehension I

Situation 1

1. How long would John like to serve as a self-supported guest researcher in the oncology department of a hospital?

   A. for two months

   B. for three months

   C. for six months

2. What did John's graduate school research project aim to do?

   A. identify prognostic factors of breast cancer

   B. elevate the curative rate for patients during treatment

   C. identify seemingly limitless medical sector opportunities

3. In what area has the hospital gained international recognition?

   A. for the ability to identify potential technical and medical sector opportunities

   B. for the ability to elevate the curative rate for patients during treatment

   C. for its own research advances

4. What reputation does the hospital that John is applying to as a guest researcher have?

   A. a sound one

   B. an excellent one

   C. a promising one

5. What field is John interested in, especially its managerial aspects?

   A. nuclear science

   B. radiology technology

   C. hospital management

Situation 2

1. How long does Mary want to serve as a guest researcher?

A. one year

B. six months

C. three months

2. Why does Mary want to gain further training at the hospital as a guest researcher?

A. owing to its commitment to excellent medical image processing as well as advanced PACS instrumentation

B. owing to its extensive training courses for technical staff in all hospital departments to maintain competitiveness

C. owing to its long tradition of commitment

3. In what capacity did Mary work in the radiology department of a hospital?

A. as a radiopharmaceutical specialist

B. as a radiochemistry professional

C. as a radiology technician

4. How did Mary further widen her exposure to the radiochemistry profession?

A. by working in the radiology department of a hospital

B. by attending several international conferences on radiology technology

C. by successfully completing both a Bachelor's degree in Radiology Technology and a Master's degree in Medical Imagery from National Tsing Hua University

5. What is Mary especially interested in researching during her guest researcher stay?

A. PET/CT-related topics

B. complex radiopharmaceutical synthesis models

C. radiopharmaceutical practices in nuclear medicine

Situation 3

1. Why does Lisa hope to serve as a self-supported guest worker?

A. to integrate diagnostic programs with the Internet and related technologies

B. to grasp the clinical implications of different diagnostic tests and operate medical instrumentation

C. to compensate for her lack of training in the picture archiving communication system (PACS)

2. What did graduate school orient on?

A. how to integrate diagnostic programs with the Internet and related technologies

B. how to easily distinguish ischemia from hemorrhaging

C. how to facilitate the diagnosis and treatment of diseases

3. What will the skills that Lisa acquired during graduate school ensure?

A. that a patient receives an accurate diagnosis

B. that a hospital possesses state-of-the-art equipment and expertise in handling stroke patients

C. that computers with valuable medical software can provide clinical physicians with data that can help determine the course of medical care

4. What highly respected training courses does the hospital that Lisa is applying to offer?

A. on creating precise anatomic images to confirm a specific malady

B. on better medical care for patients

C. on nuclear medicine

5. What is Lisa especially interested in during this training opportunity?

A. how to grasp the clinical implications of different diagnostic tests

B. how medical images facilitate the diagnosis and treatment of diseases

C. how to operate medical instrumentation appropriately

Training Application Letters
訓練申請信函

G Reading Comprehension I
Select the word or expression whose meaning is closest to the meaning of the underlined word or expression in the following passages.

Situation 1

1. Working at your company would definitely <u>promote</u> my professional development.

   A. ballyhoo

   B. occlude

   C. trammel

2. Following my gaining medical imagery expertise in graduate school, I believe that my solid academic training and practical knowledge will contribute to your company's efforts to elevate its <u>reputation</u> and new technology capabilities, even during the short three-month period at your laboratory.

   A. notoriety

   B. obloquy

   C. odium

3. As for the details of this training practicum, identifying adequate therapeutic treatment and prognostic factors is <u>essential</u> in radiology technology - a field in whose managerial aspects I am very interested.

   A. extraneous

   B. constitutive

   C. expendable

4. As for my professional interests, I have always been interested in identifying prognostic factors of breast cancer or, more specifically, those factors that can elevate the curative rate for patients during treatment. In this area of research, the potential technical and medical sector opportunities appear to be <u>limitless</u>.

A. unfathomable (correct answer)

B. hemmed in

C. precise

5. Please let me know if you require additional materials. I look forward to your <u>favorable</u> reply.

A. petulant

B. eristic

C. inclined

Situation 2

1. Through this training opportunity in your laboratory, your highly <u>skilled</u> professionals would provide me with an excellent research environment, advanced equipment and related resources to enhance my research capabilities so that I can thrive in this dynamic profession.

A. dexterous

B. invertebrate

C. spineless

2. With a long tradition of commitment, your hospital offers extensive training courses for technical staff in all hospital departments to <u>maintain</u> competitiveness.

A. disdain

B. affront

C. cultivate

3. Working in your organization, even for a short time, would definitely <u>benefit</u> my professional development.

A. stymie

B. hog-tie

C. succor

4. As for details of this <u>guest</u> internship, your department offers state-of-the-art instrumentation and clinical training of those involved in researching PET/CT-related topics.

   A. sojourner

   B. proprietor

   C. anchor man

5. Such exposure would definitely further my knowledge skills. I look forward to your thoughts regarding this proposed <u>residency</u>.

   A. instigation

   B. impetus

   C. sanctuary

Situation 3

1. Moreover, having passed an extremely difficult entrance examination for medical professionals in this field, I believe that my expertise of imagery medicine will be an <u>asset</u> to any clinical department to which I belong.

   A. arrearage

   B. boon

   C. onus

2. During this training opportunity, I will be especially interested in how medical images <u>facilitate</u> the diagnosis and treatment of diseases.

   A. assist

   B. inhibit

   C. hinder

3. In particular, computers with valuable medical software can <u>provide</u> clinical physicians with data that can help determine the course of medical care.

   A. cater

   B. dodge

C. desist

4. Training at your hospital would enable me to create precise anatomic images to <u>confirm</u> a specific malady.

    A. authenticate

    B. impugn

    C. controvert

5. Let me know if you require materials in addition to the <u>enclosed</u> resume and recommendation letters. I look forward to your favorable reply.

    A. remote

    B. clear of

    C. interpolated

H Common elements in writing a training application letter 撰寫科技訓練申請信函的通則 include the following elements:

· Request professional training. 科技訓練申請
· Summarize one's academic or professional experiences. 某人學歷及工作經驗概述
· Commend the organization to receive technical training from 讚揚提供科技訓練的機構
· Explain the details of the technical training. 科技訓練細節解釋

範例 i

Dear Professor Smith,

Allow me to introduce myself. I am a researcher in the Department of Component Technology at the Center for Measurement Standards (CMS), which is similar to ABC Institute. Educational background I am an engineer with a master's degree in Materials Science and Engineering and have received special training in thin film deposition photolithography and chemical etching. I am currently designing a process that integrates these technologies for the development of a pressure sensor that is based on a metal thin strain gauge. We plan to miniaturize this sensor in the near future.

Our laboratory would like me to receive training in micromachining technology, e.g., wet/dry silicon etching and silicon to silicon fusion bonding. I hope that your laboratory, one of the leaders in this field of research, can provide me with the opportunity to learn about sensor manufacturing technology. I wish to learn about sensor manufacturing technology at your laboratory for three months this year, preferably during March through June. Pressure sensors and related technology are what we are most concerned with. The proposed format is that of a self-supported guest worker at your laboratory.

By the way, I have an aunt living in a nearby Cupertino. Her name is Dr. Lin Mei Mei and she can be directly contacted at (408)1234567 (tel) or (408)2345678 (fax). She can provide further clarification, if necessary.

I would greatly appreciate your comments regarding this proposal. Thanks for your assistance. I look forward to our future cooperation.

In the space below, write a training application letter.

範例 ii

Dear Dr. Jones,

The Pressure/Vacuum Measurement Laboratory at the Center for Measurement Standards is planning to develop the primary pressure standard (PPS) of the mercury manometer so as to promote and strengthen our laboratory's pressure measurement capability. We have heard that your group has much experience in research involving the PPS of the mercury manometer. Would it be possible for me to serve as a guest worker in your laboratory? If granted such an opportunity, my primary objective would be to study how to design and set up the mercury manometer PPS.

Our institute, the Center for Measurement Standards, a subsidiary of the Industrial Technology Research Institute, has been entrusted with the responsibility of establishing and maintaining national standards and traceability systems. We also provide calibration services, technical consulting, and metrology training to the local industrial sector.

After reviewing your literature, I find that the systems and projects of your laboratory, especially the mercury manometer, are quite compatible with my interests. A six month period as a guest worker would probably be the most appropriate time frame. If my application is accepted, I can start no earlier than October and end no later than May 1992.

Attached please find my personal resume. Thank you for your attention to this matter.

In the space below, write a training application letter.

Look at the following example of a training application letter.

Dear Prof. Spencer, Jr.,

I would like to serve as a short-term guest researcher in the Smart Structures Technology Laboratory (SSTL) at the University of Illinois at Urbana Champaign. This self-supported research stay would be under the Graduate Student Study Abroad Program (GSSAP), as sponsored by the National Science Council of the Republic of China, Taiwan,

As seen in the enclosed resume and supporting materials, I have actively engaged in innovative structural sensor applications while pursuing a Ph.d in Civil Engineering at National Taiwan University. My current research involves monitoring (a OR the) bridge scour with smart sensing technologies. While reviewing pertinent literature, I am well aware of your innovations in structural health monitoring and smart sensor technologies. I am most eager to conduct research in a multi-cultural environment such as SSTL. I have long been intrigued with full-scale bridge health monitoring. The enclosed resume and proposal reveal that my previous academic training and employment opportunities will further add to research training received at SSTL in preparation for a career in civil engineering.

You will receive shortly recommendation letters from my advisor, Prof. Kuo-Chun Chang at the Department of Civil Engineering of National Taiwan University. If possible, I would like to be at SSTL for the period of August 2009 through July 2010.

Please let me know if you require further details not found in the enclosed materials. I look forward to your favorable reply.

Sincerely yours,

Chun-Chung Chen

Situation 4

Melody Wu

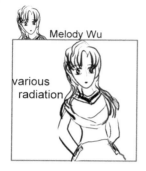

various radiation

preventive contamination injury

importance of dose detection to radiation security

Situation 5

Matt Hsiao

cancer death rate

Radiotherapy

Situation 6

John Wang

researching biology-related

journal

laboratory experience

I Write down the key points of the situations on the preceding page, while the instructor reads aloud the script from the Answer Key. Alternatively, students can listen online at www.chineseowl.idv.tw.

Situation 4

_____

_____

_____

Situation 5

_____

_____

_____

Situation 6

_____

_____

_____

J Oral practice II
Based on the three situations in this unit, write three questions beginning with **Why**, and answer them. The questions do not need to come directly from these situations.

Examples

Why would Melody like to arrange for a three-month stay as a visiting medical physicist?

because she is eager to understand the dynamic work of the cancer research center for tumor control

Why was Melody's undergraduate and graduate training in radiotechnology and medical imagery important?

because it heavily stressed close collaboration among researchers and allowed her to become adept in applying various radiation detection methods

1._____

_____

2._____

_____

3._____

_____

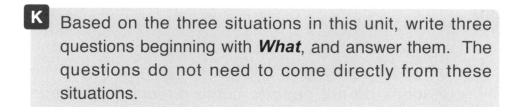

K Based on the three situations in this unit, write three questions beginning with *What*, and answer them. The questions do not need to come directly from these situations.

Examples

What would help Matt become more proficient in radiation dosimetry research?

the opportunity to serve in a self-supported guest researcher position in the laboratory that he is applying to

What did Matt's undergraduate studies in atomic physics enable him to do?

thoroughly to understand how radiation affects materials

1._____

_____

2._____

_____

3._____

_____

L Based on the three situations in this unit, write three questions beginning with **How** and answer them. The questions do not need to come directly from these situations.

Examples

How did the fundamental and advanced research capabilities that John acquired in graduate school nurture his talent?
by allowing him to approach biotechnology through a multidisciplinary approach

How was John able to immerse himself in the field of radiation? by pursuing a Master's degree in Life Sciences at National Cheng Kung University, with a particular interest in researching biology-related topics

1._____

_____

2._____

_____

3._____

_____

M   Write questions that match the answers provided.

1._____

_____

her academic and professional experiences

2._____

_____

because of his Bachelor's degree in Atomic Science and a Master's degree in
Medical Imagery

3._____

_____

the emergence of biotechnology

N Listening Comprehension II

Situation 4

1. What did Melody's undergraduate and graduate training in radiotechnology and medical imagery heavily stress?

   A. developing novel radiotherapy methods that have greatly benefited patients

   B. strict adherence to quality standards in tumor therapy

   C. close collaboration among researchers

2. What did Melody's graduate research focus on?

   A. detecting contamination during clinical practice

   B. planning appropriate radiotherapy and devising appropriate shielding for a radiotherapy room

   C. becoming proficient in the use of many radiation detection methods

3. What did Melody's academic and professional experiences increased her confidence in doing?

   A. detecting radiation dose in the workplace

   B. contributing to a patient's well-being and simultaneously maintaining radiation security

   C. planning radiological treatments and implementing radiation detection and protection strategies during therapeutic treatment

4. What evidence demonstrates how the cancer research center has distinguished itself from others in developing novel radiotherapy methods?

   A. by its strict adherence to quality standards in tumor therapy

   B. by its frequent publications in international journals

   C. by its proficiency in the use of many radiation detection methods

5. In what capacity does Melody want to contribute to a patient's well-being and simultaneously maintain radiation security?

   A. as a medical physiologist

B. as a hospital administrator

C. as a visiting researcher

Situation 5

1. How does Matt hope to become more proficient in radiation dosimetry research?

    A. by comprehending fully how seemingly opposite fields are related to each other

    B. by handling complex projects that force him to apply theoretical concepts in a practical context

    C. by serving in a self-supported guest researcher position in a laboratory

2. How does Matt view himself as an investigator in the laboratory?

    A. as a highly adept one

    B. as committed to staff excellence

    C. as capable of building on his above academic experiences

3. How has Matt greatly enhanced his competence in accumulating pertinent data and analyzing problems independently?

    A. through his Bachelor's degree in Atomic Science and a Master's degree in Medical Imagery

    B. through practical work experience

    C. through the impressive training courses that the laboratory offers

4. How did Matt become well aware of the theoretical and practical issues around radiation?

    A. through his Bachelor's degree in Atomic Science and a Master's degree in Medical Imagery

    B. through his active participation in radiation dosimetry-related projects

    C. through his intrigue with the increasing importance of radiotherapy

5. How is the laboratory's excellence in leadership and commitment to staff

excellence reflected?

A. by the way in which seemingly opposite fields are related to each other

B. the increasing importance of radiotherapy, especially given the rising cancer death rate

C. by the impressive training courses that the laboratory offers

Situation 6

1. How does John approach biotechnology?

A. by combining commercial success with innovation

B. through a multidisciplinary approach

C. by grasping fully its latest concepts

2. What was John particularly interested in researching while studying for a Master's degree in Life Sciences at National Cheng Kung University?

A. healthcare sector-related topics

B. biology-related topics

C. animal technology-related topics

3. What is an attribute that John believes the company is looking for in its research staff?

A. proficiency in biotechnology

B. an increasing emphasis on health, which accompanies an increase in the elderly population worldwide

C. a willingness to absorb tremendous amounts of information and manage my time efficiently

4. How could John further strengthen his expertise in biotechnology?

A. by using standard operating procedures to create state-of-the-art product technologies

B. by participating in the innovative research projects at the company

C. by the publishing of experimental findings in domestic and international journals

5. How did the company become a leader in the biotechnology field?

   A. by combining commercial success with innovation

   B. by creating state-of-the-art product technologies

   C. by widening its range of research interests

O Reading Comprehension II
Select the word or expression whose meaning is closest to the meaning of the underlined word or expression in the following passages.

Situation 4

1. If successful in <u>securing</u> this visiting researcher position, I will bring my professional knowledge in such areas as detecting radiation dose in the workplace, planning appropriate radiotherapy and devising appropriate shielding for a radiotherapy room.

   A. depleting

   B. chalking up

   C. ousting

2. Regarding my specific interests during this research stay, I am especially interested in the importance of dose detection to radiation <u>security</u>.

   A. chink in the armor

   B. heel of Achilles

   C. surveillance

3. This interest <u>demands</u> not only becoming proficient in the use of many radiation detection methods, but also understanding the applicability of such methods in a clinical hospital setting.

   A. stipulates

   B. remises

   C. capitulates

4. I believe that I possess the necessary <u>practical</u> and theoretical skills as a medical physiologist to contribute to a patient's well-being and simultaneously maintain radiation security.

   A. chimerical

B. speculative

C. doable

5. I believe that your organization would be an <u>excellent</u> starting point for me to begin on this career path. I look forward to your thoughts regarding this proposed stay.

A. atrocious

B. stellar

C. odious

Situation 5

1. The <u>impressive</u> training courses that your laboratory offers reflect your excellence in leadership and commitment to staff excellence.

A. formidable

B. lackluster

C. somber

2. As for the details of this proposed researcher position, I am <u>intrigued</u> with the increasing importance of radiotherapy, especially given the rising cancer death rate.

A. detached

B. assiduous

C. inattentive

3. Radiotherapy is especially attractive since it does not involve <u>injecting</u> the patient, yet yields curative effects rapidly.

A. funneling

B. inoculating

C. siphoning

4. Hopefully, by working <u>directly</u> under your supervision, I will gain further exposure to the latest techniques in this field.

A. obliquely

B. incidentally

C. verbatim

5. Please do not hesitate to contact me for an interview if this proposal is <u>feasible</u>.

A. preposterous

B. viable

C. absurd

Situation 6

1. Participating in the innovative research projects at your company would further <u>strengthen</u> my expertise in biotechnology and, hopefully, contribute to your ongoing efforts.

A. dwindle

B. rejuvenate

C. enervate

2. I am increasingly <u>drawn</u> to biotechnology, an emerging global field in the new century.

A. rebutted

B. repulsed

C. lured

3. Its <u>emergence</u> reflects an increasing emphasis on health, which accompanies an increase in the elderly population worldwide.

A. debut

B. expatriation

C. egress

4. To become proficient in this area, I must acquire further laboratory experience, explaining why I am <u>seeking</u> a valuable training opportunity at your company.

A. scaring up

B. detecting

C. delving for

5. The opportunity to work in a practicum internship in your company would provide me with an excellent environment not only to realize my career aspirations fully, but also to improve my own technological expertise. Please contact me if such an opportunity <u>arises</u>.

A. etiolates

B. ensues

C. grows dim

Unit Seven

Employment Recommendation Letters

就業推薦信函

· Introduction and qualification to make recommendation
撰寫推薦信函（A部分）推薦信函開始及推薦人的資格

· Recommending a student for study (Part B): Personal qualities of the applicant relevant to employment and Closing
撰寫推薦信函（B 部分）被推薦人與進階學習有關的個人特質及信函結尾

Vocabulary and related expressions

globally renowned corporation	全球知名企業
endless perseverance	不屈不撓的韌性（毅力）
tedious and detailed tasks	單調乏味的事務細節
diligence in collecting and organizing materials	奮戰不懈地收集、組合材料
understands the limitations of conventional research	領悟傳統研究的束縛
solve problems from various angles	從各種角度解決問題
gain professional competence	獲得專業能力
eminent organization	高知名度的組織
work diligently to develop one's natural talents	勤奮工作開發某人的天分
task at hand	手邊任務
delve into	探索（探究）……
synthesize pertinent reading	綜合相關讀物
innovative technology developments	創新科技發展
foster one's fundamental research skills	培養某人的基本研究技巧
logical competence	邏輯能力
identify potential solutions	指出可能的解決方案
equip one with academic fundamentals	讓某人具備學業基礎
intensely competitive hi-tech sector	高度競爭的高科技產業
widely respected throughout the company	普遍受到全公司上下的敬重
exemplary communication and leadership skills	溝通和領導技巧可作為別人的楷模
refined coordinating skills and direct communication style	純熟的整合技巧和直接溝通的風格
simplifying administrative procedures	簡化管理程序（流程）
spearhead	先鋒（前鋒）
provide further insight into	進一步洞悉……
resourceful individual	足智多謀的人
filling out weekly progress reports	填寫週進度報告
derive complex models	衍生複雜的模型
widen one's professional exposure	擴大某人的專業度
unforeseen bottlenecks in research	始料未及的研究瓶頸
strong personality traits	強烈的個性特質
ability to grasp abstract concepts quickly	迅速掌握抽象概念的能力
willingness to accept others' constructive criticism	願意接納別人建設性的批評
examine a diverse array of topics	檢驗各種主題
identify demographic variables	辨別人口變數
bottlenecks in production	量產的瓶頸
adeptness in generating beneficial results	擅長催生有利的結果

Situation 1

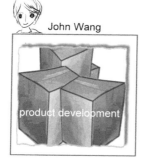

John Wang

product development

Mary

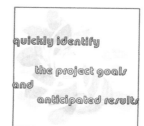

quickly identify the project goals and anticipated results

Situation 2

Professor Lisa Lu

Jerry Su

reading and investigating

reading and investigating

unique perspective

Situation 3

Professor Jason Ling

Matt Chen

school

workplace effectively

Matt Chen

definitely allow

Employment Recommendation Letters
就業推薦信函

A Write down the key points of the situations on the preceding page, while the instructor reads aloud the script from the Answer Key. Alternatively, students can listen online at www.chineseowl.idv.tw.

Situation 1

_____

_____

_____

Situation 2

_____

_____

_____

Situation 3

_____

_____

_____

B Oral practice I
Based on the three situations in this unit, write three questions beginning with **What**, and answer them. The questions do not need to come directly from these situations.

Examples

What qualifies John to recommend Mary for employment?

He supervised her in the product development group for the past two years.

What has undoubtedly enabled Mary to improve her knowledge skills continuously?

her proactive approach towards learning

1. _____

_____

2. _____

_____

3. _____

_____

C Based on the three situations in this unit, write three questions beginning with **Why**, and answer them. The questions do not need to come directly from these situations.

Examples

Why is Jerry's unique ability to integrate and explain seemingly contradictory concepts to those outside of his field of expertise invaluable in the workplace?

because it can help provide enough details to managers to enable them to make management decisions based on that information

Why is it a marvelous opportunity for Jerry to secure employment in this eminent organization?

so that he can gain professional competence

1._____

_____

2._____

_____

3._____

_____

D Based on the three situations in this unit, write three questions beginning with **How**, and answer them. The questions do not need to come directly from these situations.

Examples

How does Matt's graduate school advisor rank him in terms of implementing the organization's innovative technology developments?

as the most qualified individual

How does Matt approach the task set before him?

methodically and thoroughly

1._____

_____

2._____

_____

3._____

_____

E Write questions that match the answers provided.

1._____

_____

weekly

2._____

_____

since graduation

3._____

_____

a career in industrial management

F Listening Comprehension I

Situation 1

1. What is Mary's seemingly endless perseverance in handling tedious and detailed tasks evidence of?

   A. her proactive approach

   B. her energy

   C. her diligence

2. How has Mary been able to improve her knowledge skills continuously?

   A. through her creativity and cooperative nature

   B. through her exemplary analytical skills

   C. through her proactive approach towards learning

3. How did Mary play an important role in product development efforts?

   A. by collecting and organizing materials within the laboratory

   B. by helping to improve the living standard of customers

   C. by analyzing the most pertinent information and then quickly identifying the project goals and anticipated results

4. What was Mary's approach when undertaking numerous experiments?

   A. She actively participated, offering carefully composed questions and responses to other group members.

   B. She analyzed the most pertinent information and then quickly identified the project goals and anticipated results.

   C. She attempted to solve problems from various angles.

5. What did weekly group meetings often involve?

   A. performing various experimental procedures and analyzing the results

   B. discussion of journals and case reports (correct answer)

   C. identifying exactly what is required for a particular research objective

Situation 2

1. Why is Professor Lu in a good position to assess Jerry?

    A. because she supervised his doctoral level research and dissertation as his academic advisor

    B. because she actively participated with him in several National Science Council-sponsored research projects

    C. because she helped him to develop his natural talents, during which, she displayed seemingly endless energy

2. How can integrating and explaining seemingly contradictory concepts to those outside of his field of expertise be invaluable in the workplace?

    A. It can help to identify fellow classmates' needs and incorporate their opinions in forming laboratory policies.

    B. It can help to maintain contact with several researchers in the field, discussing issues relating to their clinical or research experience.

    C. It can help provide enough details to managers to enable them to make management decisions based on that information.

3. What attributes will undoubtedly support Jerry's future employment?

    A. his maturity and diligence

    B. his intelligence, industry and dedication

    C. strong analytical skills and sound ability to formulate opinions after synthesizing available knowledge

4. How has Jerry continued to maintain contact with several researchers in the field?

    A. by discussing issues relating to their clinical or research experience

    B. by synthesizing pertinent reading, identifying limitations of previous literature and then stating the logical next step from a unique perspective

    C. by identifying fellow classmates' needs and incorporating their opinions in forming laboratory policies

5. What evidence points to Jerry's remarkable critical thinking skills?

  A. his strong analytical skills and sound ability to formulate opinions after synthesizing available knowledge

  B. his natural talents

  C. his ability to synthesize pertinent reading, identify limitations of previous literature and then state the logical next step from a unique perspective

Situation 3

1. What two adjectives describe Matt's personality?

  A. confident and collaborative

  B. methodical and thorough

  C. straightforward and rigorous

2. How did the graduate curriculum markedly differ from Matt's undergraduate curriculum?

  A. It involved learning how to analyze problems, identify potential solutions, and implement those solutions according to concepts taught in the classroom.

  B. It equipped him not only with the academic fundamentals required for a management-related career, but also with the workplace skills to meet the rigorous challenges of the intensely competitive hi-tech sector.

  C. It offered many opportunities for him to strengthen his research fundamentals.

3. What is Matt committed to?

  A. solving problems logically and straightforwardly

  B. pursuing a career in industrial management

  C. fostering his fundamental research skills

4. What are two of Matt's attributes that will the company find attractive?

  A. his intuition when adapting to new environments and diligence in the task at hand

B. much knowledge and logical competence to address problems in the workplace effectively

C. academic fundamentals required for a management-related career and workplace skills to meet the rigorous challenges of the intensely competitive hi-tech sector

5. What is Matt deeply interested in?

A. a management-related career

B. professional expertise in industrial management

C. quality control

G Reading Comprehension I
Select the word or expression whose meaning is closest to the meaning of the underlined word or expression in the following passages.

Situation 1

1. Furthermore, her analytical skills are <u>exemplary</u>.

   A. quintessential

   B. culpable

   C. censurable

2. Although occasionally unfamiliar with a particular technology development at the <u>outset</u>, she would analyze the most pertinent information and then quickly identify the project goals and anticipated results.

   A. termination

   B. cessation

   C. induction

3. I have no <u>qualms</u> in recommending this highly motivated individual for employment in your organization.

   A. scruples

   B. convictions

   C. credence

4. Her creativity and cooperative nature will be a great asset to any future product development effort in which she is <u>involved</u>.

   A. severed

   B. enmeshed

   C. disjoined

5. Your corporation's great working environment, combined with the impressive number and <u>diversity</u> of training courses to maintain the competence of

its employees in the market place, would definitely ensure the ongoing development of Mary's professional skills while helping to improve the living standard of your customers.

   A. monotony

   B. heterogeneity

   C. analogy

Situation 2

1. For instance, whenever encountering a research bottleneck, he <u>consistently</u> delved into reading and investigating the source of the problem while consulting with me on how to solve it.

   A. transiently

   B. invariably

   C. momentarily

2. Since graduation, he has <u>continued</u> to maintain contact with several researchers in the field, discussing issues relating to their clinical or research experience.

   A. interposed

   B. suspended

   C. abided

3. In addition, his critical thinking skills are remarkable, as evidenced by his ability to synthesize pertinent reading, identify limitations of previous literature and then state the <u>logical</u> next step from a unique perspective.

   A. incongruous

   B. perspicuous

   C. preposterous

4. I do not hesitate in most highly <u>recommending</u> Jerry for employment in your organization.

   A. renouncing

B. vouching for

C. scoffing

5. Do not <u>hesitate</u> to contact me if I can provide you with any further insight into this highly qualified individual.

A. edge forward

B. progress

C. vacillate

Situation 3

1. At graduate school, while learning how to adopt different perspectives in <u>approaching</u> a particular problem during undergraduate training, he acquired several statistical and analytical skills.

A. tergiversating

B. verging upon

C. seceding

2. Doing so involved learning how to analyze problems, identify potential <u>solutions,</u> and implement those solutions according to concepts taught in the classroom.

A. quandaries

B. quick fixes

C. plights

3. The graduate school curricula equipped him not only with the academic <u>fundamentals</u> required for a management-related career, but also with the workplace skills to meet the rigorous challenges of the intensely competitive hi-tech sector.

A. accessories

B. contingencies

C. meat-and-potatoes

4. Securing employment in your company would definitely allow him to <u>realize</u> fully his career aspirations.

A. discern

B. warp

C. contort

5. I am quite <u>confident</u> of Matt's ability to contribute significantly to any collaborative effort in which he is involved in your company.

A. speculative

B. sanguine

C. ambivalent

H Common elements in writing an employment recommendation letter 撰寫求職推薦信函的通則 include the following elements:

· Introduction and qualification to make recommendation 撰寫推薦信函（A部分）推薦信函開始及推薦人的資格
· Recommending an individual for employment (Part B): Personal qualities of the applicant relevant to employment and Closing 撰寫推薦信函（B部分）被推薦人與進階學習有關的個人特質及信函結尾

Introduction and qualification to make recommendation

I became acquainted with her in a promotional event on campus three years ago. As the contact for this event, she coordinated a market research survey for our company.

As a diligent and enthusiastic student whom I have known for over four years, Mr. Johnny Li enrolled in several of my classes offered at National Taiwan University, including Introduction to Commerce, Strategic Management and Marketing Theory. Also serving as Miss Fang's graduate school advisor, I wholeheartedly recommend her for employment in your organization.

Given my considerable industrial experience, I feel that I am qualified to highly recommend her for employment in your company.

Personal qualities of the applicant relevant to employment

Her intuitiveness towards the latest marketing trends has made her stand out among her appears despite her youth.

With her tremendous potential, her talents will be continuously refined when actively engaging in your company's many collaborative efforts.

As evidence of her academic excellence, Mr. Li completed an exhaustive doctoral dissertation on consumer trends in Taiwan's semiconductor industry. He accumulated a tremendous amount of data from local and overseas studies, applying it to a thorough introduction and analysis of the latest developments in this hi-tech industry. I was especially impressed with her outstanding oral defense, highlighted by her ability to clearly express well thought out opinions within a time limit

Closing

Based on his exemplary credentials, I hold no qualms in highly recommending Mr Li for employment in your company. Such an opportunity would allow him to benefit from the excellent resources that your corporate structure offers. Please do not hesitate to contact me if I can provide further insight into this highly qualified candidate.

In the space below, write an employment recommendation letter

_____

_____

_____

_____

_____

_____

_____

_____

_____

_____

Look at the following examples of an employment recommendation letter.

範例 i

I have encouraged Matt Chen to seek employment in your research institute for quite some time. As his graduate school advisor, I cannot think of a more qualified individual to receive exposure to your organization's innovative technological developments to further his career.

Matt is methodical and thorough in any task set before him, regardless of whether it is academic or professional. Graduate study equipped him with the required knowledge and fundamental professional expertise in industrial management. The graduate curriculum markedly differed from his undergraduate curriculum, offering many opportunities for him to strengthen his research fundamentals. For instance, the theoretical and practical concepts taught in the graduate curriculum increased his ability to solve problems logically and straightforwardly. Additionally, the theoretical knowledge and practical laboratory experience gained at graduate school were equally important in allowing him to foster his fundamental research skills. Given his deep interest in quality control, he is committed to pursuing a career in industrial management. In summary, graduate school equipped him with much knowledge and logical competence to address problems in the workplace effectively - an attribute that your research institute will find a most valuable one.

I am also impressed with Matt's intuition when adapting to new environments. At graduate school, while learning how to adopt different perspectives in approaching a particular problem during undergraduate training, he acquired several statistical and analytical skills. Doing so involved learning how to analyze problems, identify potential solutions, and implement those solutions based on concepts taught in the classroom. The graduate school curricula equipped him not only with the academic fundamentals required for a management-related career, but also with the workplace skills required to meet the rigorous challenges of the intensely competitive hi-tech sector. Receiving advanced training in your research institute would definitely enable him to realize fully his career aspirations.

I am quite confident of Matt's ability to contribute significantly to any collaborative effort in which he is involved in your institute. Please contact me if I can be of further assistance.

Yours truly,

Professor Mike Meyer

Sincerely yours,

Chun-Chung Chen

Situation 4

Mary Kuan

refined coordinating skills and direct communication style

marketing-related decisions

Susan Chuang

reducing administrative costs and the number of personne

Situation 5

Jerry Su

resourceful

John Chang

innovative

innovative

higher standards

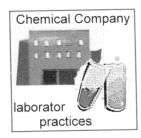

Chemical Company

laborator practices

Situation 6

Julianne Wang

Kelly Lin

Julianne Wang

strong interpersonal relation

factory production line

I Write down the key points of the situations on the preceding page, while the instructor reads aloud the script from the Answer Key. Alternatively, students can listen online at www.chineseowl.idv.tw.

Situation 4

_____

_____

_____

Situation 5

_____

_____

_____

Situation 6

_____

_____

_____

J Oral practice II

Based on the three situations in this unit, write three questions beginning with **Why**, and answer them. The questions do not need to come directly from these situations.

Examples

Why is Susan widely respected throughout the company?

Her group leader often said so.

Why has Susan facilitated the smooth implementation of several events and company policies?

owing to her refined coordinating skills and direct communication style

1. _____

_____

2. _____

_____

3. _____

_____

K Based on the three situations in this unit, write three questions beginning with *How*, and answer them. The questions do not need to come directly from these situations.

Examples

How did Jerry become familiar with John?

John has been an associate researcher at the laboratory under Jerry's supervision for the past five years.

How does Jerry characterize John?

as a resourceful individual

1._____

_____

2._____

_____

3._____

_____

L Based on the three situations in this unit, write three questions beginning with **What**, and answer them. The questions do not need to come directly from these situations.

Examples

What is Kelly willing to accept in order to be more effective in an assigned task? others' constructive criticism

What does Julianne view Kelly's unique characteristic as? the ability to examine a diverse array of topics and, then, search for their possible relationship in the workplace to increase productivity

1._____

_____

2._____

_____

3._____

_____

M Write questions that match the answers provided.

1._____

_____

Susan's professional experience and knowledge skills

2._____

_____

when first entering the laboratory

3._____

_____

monitoring the manufacturing capacity of the factory production line

N Listening Comprehension II

Situation 4

1. In what capacity did Mary Kuan observe Susan Chuang?

    A. as departmental supervisor

    B. as group leader

    C. as graduate school advisor

2. What are two personal qualities of Susan that impressed Mary Kuan with respect to her pursuit of a management career?

    A. her passion and resolve

    B. her refined coordinating skills and direct communication style

    C. strong desire to improve her research capabilities and her active participation in a collaborative project

3. What will definitely prove to be a valuable asset to the company that Susan is applying to?

    A. her strong desire to improve her research capabilities

    B. her strong leadership potential

    C. her adaptability

4. What did Susan spearhead in Mary's department?

    A. a collaborative project for our company, in which she analyzed customer data

    B. accumulation of customer data in a novel database for statistical software purposes

    C. development of a novel administrative procedure for classifying and simplifying customers' financial information

5. What will enable Susan to easily blend into your product development team's innovative efforts?

    A. her professional experience and knowledge skills

B. her strong desire to improve her research capabilities

C. her adaptability

Situation 5

1. What is an example of John's resourcefulness?

A. He derived complex models and modified laboratory practices to meet a specific research requirement.

B. He quickly learned how to coordinate different aspects of a research project.

C. He extended his knowledge skills to fields outside his academic studies to provide innovative solutions.

2. How was John able to extend his knowledge skills to fields outside his academic studies to provide innovative solutions?

A. by actively participating in many process development-related projects

B. by participating in several of the laboratory's research projects

C. by responding effectively to unforeseen bottlenecks in research

3. How was John able to respond effectively to unforeseen bottlenecks in research?

A. by undertaking intensive laboratory training

B. by meeting a specific research requirement

C. by managing financial affairs or organizing regularly held seminars and report contents

4. How did John further widen his professional exposure?

A. by actively participating in many process development-related projects

B. by continuously striving for higher standards

C. by attending several international conferences

5. How did John acquire advanced knowledge skills as a chemical engineer at Johnson Chemical Company?

A. by continuously striving for higher standards

B. by participating in many process development-related projects

C. by deriving complex models and modifying laboratory practices to meet a specific research requirement

Situation 6

1. What does Kelly have the unique characteristic of doing?

A. examining a diverse array of topics and, then, searching for their possible relationship in the workplace to increase productivity

B. easily adjusting to various organizational positions

C. identifying effective demographic variables and forecasting accurately growth trends of the company's products and services.

2. What has Julianne Wang been responsible for doing at the company over the past four years?

A. assessing Kelly's ability to meet the rigorous work demands of a research team

B. reviewing Kelly's initiation of a similar project aimed at developing an efficient product control system

C. evaluating Kelly's work performance evaluations

3. What reaffirms Julianne's conviction that flexibility is essential to strong interpersonal relations?

A. the fact that Kelly is adept in generating beneficial results that will contribute to corporate revenues

B. the fact that Kelly easily adjusts to various organizational positions

C. the fact that Kelly can estimate consumer demand in the hi-tech sector

4. Why is Julianne in a unique position?

A. She can assess Kelly's strong commitment to the marketing profession.

B. She can assess Kelly's character and willingness to collaborate closely with other colleagues.

C. She can assess Kelly's ability to meet the rigorous work demands of your research team.

5. Why will Kelly be able to contribute to corporate revenues?

A. owing to her ability to monitor the manufacturing capacity of our factory production line

B. owing to her adeptness in generating beneficial results

C. owing to her ability to identify effective demographic variables and forecast accurately growth trends

Reading Comprehension II
Select the word or expression whose meaning is closest
to the meaning of the underlined word or expression in
the following passages.

Situation 4

1. Carefully analyzing the data revealed <u>unique</u> facts about the company's
   particular circumstances, which provided valuable references for administrators
   who had to make marketing-related decisions.

   A. dime-a-dozen

   B. anomalous

   C. garden-variety

2. In a similar development, Susan spearheaded our department's development
   of a novel administrative procedure for classifying and <u>simplifying</u> customers'
   financial information, processed by our company's accounting division.

   A. muddling

   B. convoluting

   C. abridging

3. A database containing detailed customer information is accessed while ensuring
   the <u>confidentiality</u> of such information, thus reducing administrative costs and
   the number of personnel involved.

   A. guilelessness

   B. clandestineness

   C. veracity

4. I, therefore, have no <u>hesitation</u> in strongly recommending this individual to
   your corporate family.

   A. oscillation

   B. moxie

C. tenacity

5. Your Human Resources Department is <u>welcome</u> to contact me for further insight into this highly qualified candidate.

A. jettisoned

B. disdained

C. embraced

Situation 5

1. After receiving a Bachelor's degree in Chemistry from National Chung Hsing University in 1993, he <u>secured</u> employment as a chemical engineer at Johnson Chemical Company.

A. procured

B. relinquished

C. expended

2. In this capacity, he acquired <u>advanced</u> knowledge skills by actively participating in many process development-related projects.

A. sluggish

B. dilatory

C. cutting edge

3. He later joined Dupree Chemical Company in 1996, where he served as senior engineer <u>responsible</u> for process control.

A. culpable

B. fly-by-night

C. devil-may-care

4. I believe that you will find such experience to be valuable to your highly <u>qualified</u> staff.

A. neophyte

B. bush league

C. catechized

5. I fully <u>endorse</u> John in his desire to work in your company.

   A. stigmatize

   B. champion

   C. derogate

Situation 6

1. Kelly also initiated a similar project aimed at developing an efficient product control system capable of <u>monitoring</u> the manufacturing capacity of our factory production line.

   A. auditing

   B. disdaining

   C. slighting

2. The system subsequently developed by her team not only evaluates precisely bottlenecks in production, but also determines <u>immediately</u> the current output and efficiency of the production line.

   A. downstream

   B. ulterior

   C. pronto

3. Her success in these projects reflects her <u>adeptness</u> in generating beneficial results that will contribute to corporate revenues, an attribute which I believe that your company is seeking.

   A. oafishness

   B. proficiency

   C. uncouthness

4. I am highly confident of Kelly's ability to meet the <u>rigorous</u> work demands of your research team.

   A. derelict

B. slipshod

C. scrupulous

5. As your company offers a competitive work environment for highly skilled professionals, I believe that she will be a welcome <u>addition</u> to your corporate family.

A. excision

B. augmentation

C. abatement

Answer Key

解 答

Answer Key
Problem Analysis Reports
問題分析報告

A

Situation 1

During our most recent board meeting, participants expressed concern over the current tendency of financial institutions to underrate a company's value by failing to consider intellectual capital assets, which dominate in enterprises such as online gaming companies. As the global economy moves into the information age, knowledge is the most fundamental intangible capital asset and will increasingly dominate efforts to create a competitive edge and generate wealth. Although tangible assets such as property, facilities, and equipment continue to be critical to the manufacturing of products and providing services, their relative importance has declined as the importance of intellectual capital has increased. Intellectual capital includes inventions, ideas, general know-how, design approaches, computer programs, processes and publications. Although capable of measuring the value of tangible assets that can be quantified in a company, conventional accounting methods do not include intellectual capital, and therefore underrate a company's value. Therefore determining exactly how an organization should assess its intellectual competency is a priority. Additionally, scientific and technological advances have heightened the importance of intellectual capital, as evidenced by the numerous companies that rely almost completely on intellectual assets for generating revenue. For instance, on-line gaming companies emphasize the ownership of intangible capital rather than tangible assets. Online gaming ranks at the top of the gaming industry, with generated revenues of US$1 billion in 1999, skyrocketing to US$2 billion in 2002. According to the International Data Corporation (2003), in 2002, the on-line gaming market was 533,000,000 units in the Asian Pacific region, with South Korea and Taiwan leading the way, accounting for 54% and 26%, respectively. The inability to measure the value of companies without incorporating intellectual capital not only leads to an underrating of their value, but also prevents an understanding of how intellectual capital affects the on-line gaming market. Therefore, a novel index based on the analysis hierarchy process (AHP) must be developed to determine the value of the intellectual capital of on-line gaming companies.

Situation 2

At a recent meeting, members discussed the increasing incidence of outstanding debts and a higher risk of defaulting on loans owing to substandard lending practices. The increasing popularity of credit cards in Taiwan has led to serious domestic competition. Banks encourage prospective customers to hold multiple credit cards by relaxing approval and credit reference procedures. However, such practices have significantly undermined the creditworthiness of issuing banks. Few studies have measured varying degrees of risk among potential credit card customers to identify both varying degrees of risk and reasons for credit card debt. The severity of this problem is indicated by the fact that the average Taiwanese has an average of 2.8 cards from the currently available 6,321 credit cards available domestically, with credit card debt at 46% of the credit limit. The inability to identify either the degree of risk or the reasons for credit card debt will further exacerbate the bank lending crisis in Taiwan, ultimately threatening the survival of credit cooperatives owing to the inability to control effectively the spiraling of outstanding debts. Therefore, a novel evaluation method must be developed to identify credit card customers that incorporate the characteristics associated with the lifestyles of such customers and factors that contribute to easily incurred debts.

Situation 3

In our working group meeting of last week, we discussed our hospital's difficulty in retaining current patients and reducing the turnover rate of patients who go to other medical centers for treatment. The extremely competitive medical market sector in Taiwan and budget deficits caused by the island's National Health Insurance scheme have led to the implementation of a Global Budget System. Although hospitals prioritize attracting new patients, patient turnover rate has been receiving increasing attention. Hospitals must concentrate their operational effort on retaining current patients and reducing the turnover rate of those who are going to other medical centers for treatment. In the relatively few studies that have addressed this area, conventional approaches calculate the number of patients on a daily basis without differentiating between new and return patients. Incapable of determining patient turnover rates precisely, our hospital could face considerable expense in attracting new patients in the face of shrinking subsidies from the National Health Insurance scheme, ultimately lowering our competitiveness. The inability to address effectively patient turnover rate makes the statistical approaches used to determine the samples in pertinent studies inaccurate. Therefore, a novel prediction model must be developed to identify the turnover rate of customers in the medical sector. Administrators should incorporate a novel set of management strategies that emphasize customer retention within the medical sector.

B

1. Why do conventional accounting methods underrate a company's value?
   They do not include intellectual capital.

2. Why is an understanding of how intellectual capital affects the on-line gaming market impossible?
   owing to the inability to measure the value of companies without incorporating intellectual capital not only leads to an underrating of their value

3. Why must researchers develop a novel index based on the analysis hierarchy

process (AHP)?

to determine the value of the intellectual capital of on-line gaming companies

C

1. How has the creditworthiness of issuing banks become significantly undermined?

owing to conventional lending practices

2. How is the severity of this creditworthiness problem demonstrated?

by the fact that the average Taiwanese has an average of 2.8 cards from the currently available 6,321 credit cards available domestically, with credit card debt at 46% of the credit limit

3. How is the survival of credit cooperatives ultimately threatened?

owing to the inability to control effectively the spiraling of outstanding debts

D

1. What do conventional approaches fail to differentiate between? new and return patients

2. What makes the statistical approaches used to determine the samples in pertinent studies inaccurate?

the inability to address effectively patient turnover rate

3. What should management strategies emphasize?

customer retention within the medical sector

E

1. What is the global economy moving into?

2. Why will the bank lending crisis in Taiwan be further exacerbated?

3. What must hospitals concentrate their operational effort on?

Answer Key
Problem Analysis Reports
問題分析報告

F

Situation 1

1. B   2. C   3. B   4. A   5. C

Situation 2

1. C   2. B   3. B   4. A   5. C

Situation 3

1. B   2. B   3. C   4. C   5. B

G

Situation 1

1. B   2. B   3. A   4. C   5. B

Situation 2

1. B   2. C   3. A   4. C   5. A

Situation 3

1. C   2. A   3. A   4. C   5. C

I

Situation 4

Hospital administrators recently expressed concern over how to select the most qualified vendor for handling medical waste produced by our facility. Taiwanese hospitals must effectively cope with not only the severe budgetary constraints of the national health insurance scheme, but also stringent mandates on medical waste treatment from the Environmental Protection Administration. While hospitals dispose of large amounts of medical waste to ensure sanitation and personal hygiene, doing so creates potential environmental hazards and increases operating expenses. The environmental protection sector is just beginning to address harmful waste emitted by the waste treatment sector, largely because of the lack of effective management experience in closely monitoring daily operations. However, the scope of services that medical waste disposal firms provide does not always meet the needs of individual hospitals. While the ability to handle medical waste efficiently depends on the ability of hospitals to adopt sound waste management practices and coordinate their efforts with waste disposal firms, Taiwanese hospitals lack an objective criterion for selecting the most appropriate waste disposal firm and evaluating its performance, but rely on their own subjective judgment and previous experience. According to Department of Health statistics, approximately 17,500 hospital clinics, operating domestically with a bed capacity of roughly 120,000, produce nearly 300 metric tons of medical waste daily, of which 15% is infectious, which value is increasing. Given the growth in medical waste, the inability of hospitals to adopt an objective means of evaluating a waste disposal firm and its performance may lead to inappropriate selection and higher operational costs, necessitating the development of an effective means of objectively evaluating the performance of waste disposal firms, thus reducing overhead costs and improving medical waste management. Since most hospitals contract waste disposal firms to handle their waste, administrators need a reliable method for contracting the most appropriate firm to monitor closely and reduce expenditures associated with this process.

Situation 5

At a recent meeting, members discussed ways to enhance the performance of hospitals so that administrators can revise management direction based on analytic methods that accurately reflect the efficiency of the healthcare services they provide. Rapid changes in Taiwan's healthcare environment have led to a limitation of medical resources that make efficient distribution essential. Efficient distribution is a priority of health organizations. State-level administrators should analyze the productivity of each hospital to determine whether resources are being utilized effectively. In many countries, the public sector, rather than non-profit organizations, provides most of the commercial and social services, making their contribution extremely difficult to measure using conventional aggregative performance indicators such as return on investment (ROI), residual income (RI) and profitability. All hospitals utilize resources to provide many services, which are the output of healthcare organizations. Thus, the efficiency with which inputs are used to produce these services is an important measure of performance. Of the 14,474 public and private medical institutions that were operating in Taiwan as of the end of 1992, public medical care institutions comprised 97 hospitals and 479 clinics while private institutions comprised 728 hospitals and 13,170 clinics. Given the substantial investment made by governments in healthcare, the efficiency of public hospitals is a priority. The inability to measure this efficiency almost prevents the allocation of medical resources to hospitals by government. An analysis must be based not only on the efficiency of healthcare services offered by public hospitals, as determined using data envelopment analysis (DEA), but also on those factors that enhance the performance of hospitals such that administrators can revise directions in management accordingly.

Situation 6

Our hospital administrators recently expressed concern over how to evaluate outsourced nursing care attendants to select the most productive outsourcing agencies. A rapidly growing elderly population poses a major challenge for long-term care management, which requires immediate solutions, given changing family structures and the frequency of chronic illnesses. Almost all employees in hospital-subsidized respiratory care centers, respiratory care wards and nursing homes, are nursing care attendants. In a sub-specialist field at a medical department, nursing care attendants do not hold a specialized license nor have all reached a certain academic level. They simply require basic healthcare training skills and knowledge of hospital or governmental infrastructure to perform their tasks efficiently. Playing an important role in Taiwanese society, nursing care attendants accompany disabled individuals and provide assistance with daily activities such as taking a bath, eating meals, monitoring urinary or stool specimens, changing the posture of incapacitated stroke victims and providing general comfort. Despite their contributions, most nursing care attendants lack a uniform management approach to ensure the quality of service. They have no restrictions of age, education or experience - but must be mentally and physically healthy. Despite the abundance of outsourcing agencies for nursing care attendants, the lack of standardized training prevents control of the quality of service provided island-wide. Moreover, changes in Taiwan's National Health Insurance scheme have led to an emphasis on controlling personnel costs while maintaining high-quality services, further contributing to the outsourcing of nursing care attendants.

Generally, relatives or patients directly employ a nursing care attendant without adequate evaluative criteria to select the most appropriate care provider. Additionally, outsourcing firms lack objective criteria for selecting nursing care attendants, leading to widespread customer dissatisfaction and increasing management difficulty. Given the 22 hospital subsidized nursing homes and 18 respiratory care wards currently operating in Taiwan, the importance of nursing care attendants is obvious. The inability to manage effectively the quality of service that nursing care attendants provide will lead to a further decline in hospital revenues, and eventually to a reduction in personnel and community services. Therefore, a selection model based on fuzzy theory and the AHP method must be developed, capable of providing an objective means of evaluating the quality of nursing care attendants and, ultimately, enhancing the quality of service, increasing customer satisfaction and lowering personnel costs.

J

1. Why are potential environmental hazards created and operating expenses increased?

   because hospitals dispose of large amounts of medical waste to ensure sanitation and personal hygiene

2. Why is the environmental protection sector just beginning to address harmful waste emitted by the waste treatment sector? largely because of the lack of effective management experience in closely monitoring daily operations

3. Why do Taiwanese hospitals rely on their own subjective judgment and previous experience when selecting the most appropriate waste disposal firm and evaluating its performance?

   because they lack an objective criterion

K

1. What is an important measure of hospital performance?

   the efficiency with which inputs are used to produce healthcare services

2. What almost prevents the government from allocating medical resources to hospitals?

   the inability to measure the efficiency of healthcare services

3. What should state-level administrators analyze to determine whether resources are being utilized effectively?

   the productivity of each hospital

L

1. How do nursing care attendants play an important role in Taiwanese society?

   They accompany disabled individuals and provide assistance with daily activities.

2. How have widespread customer dissatisfaction and increasing management difficulty occurred?

Outsourcing firms lack objective criteria for selecting nursing care attendants.

3. How do relatives or patients generally employ a nursing care attendant?

without adequate evaluative criteria to select the most appropriate care provider.

M

1. How much waste do 17,500 hospital clinics operating domestically produce?

2. How many public and private medical institutions were operating in Taiwan as of the end of 1992?

3. What do most nursing care attendants lack?

N

Situation 4

1. B   2. B   3. C   4. C   5. B

Situation 5

1. B   2. C   3. B   4. C   5. A

Situation 6

1. B   2. C   3. A   4. C   5. B

O

Situation 4

1. A   2. C   3. B   4. A   5. B

Situation 5

1. A   2. C   3. A   4. A   5. B

Situation 6

1. C   2. A   3. B   4. A   5. C

Answer Key
Recommendation Reports
調查性與建議性報告

A

Situation 1

Members of our working group recently raised the concern that, with respect to differentiated marketing practices in Taiwan, conventional methods of ranking customers are normally based on bank account balances in each accounting period. This basis alone does not provide a complete customer profile, and seldom supports strategies that analyze the commercial transaction data of customers. Insufficient information on unique customer characteristics prevents the provision of services specialized for individuals. The inability to interact compatibly with customers will cause our company to lose its focus on product development and promotional strategies. Therefore, we recommend developing a customer ranking model by analyzing the dynamic purchasing behavior of customers and identifying those who have the potential to generate bank revenues. Those behavioral results can be used to devise diverse promotional strategies or customize products or services according to consumer needs, achieving market differentiation and effective customer relations. Based on numerous available customer data, a data mining method, CRISP-DM, which combines the conventional means of data exploration with two mathematical calculations (decision tree and category nerve) can be adopted to determine how various purchasing activities are related and how many factors are involved in evaluating a customer's relationship. These factors include the types of products purchased, their quantity and their cost of acquisition and servicing. Factors associated with customer relations and customer life cycle can then be combined to construct an enhanced management model. In the proposed model, factors of the ranking module are verified and adjusted to ensure that a company continuously provides quality services. The customer's value in customer relationship management can be determined, and the model significantly enhances the company's ability to attract new customers. Furthermore, this model can be used in other business sectors to enhance the identification, acquisition and retention of loyal and profitable customers.

Situation 2

Taiwan's growing elderly population has increased the demand for long-term healthcare facilities and services. While forecasting the medical market trends (both in supply and demand) is a fundamental part of feasibility analysis, both governmental makers of social welfare policy and commercial investors rely heavily on forecasts to remain abreast of regulations that govern health financing and the development of new projects. Whereas the modeling method has seldom been adopted to forecast market trends in long-term care in Taiwan, most studies have focused on various consumer indexes used to forecast the market supply and demand but neglect the market and natural factors that affect the long-term healthcare sector. Therefore, we recommend the development of two forecasting models to estimate the demand of the elderly population in Taiwan for the available long-term healthcare resources. A multi-regression model can be developed to measure and forecast not only the quantity of early demand, but also the relationship between the demand and critical factors by accumulating a significant amount of data and identifying such factors. The data can then be collected using a questionnaire, with the factors quantitatively measured using a method found in the literature. Next, a GM (1, 1) model based on Grey Theory can be developed to accurately forecast the supply of available long-term healthcare resources from data acquired from the website of Taiwan's Ministry of Interior. In addition to identifying factors that affect the demand, the proposed forecasting models can also measure precisely the demand for and supply of long-term healthcare resources in Taiwan. The proposed forecasting models provide a valuable reference for makers of health-care policy, investors in the medical sector, administrators and academics, when devising relevant policies and strategies.

Situation 3

Purchasing on credit is increasingly common in Taiwan, as evidenced by the rise in customer loans granted by local banks in recent years. When processing loan applications, the banking officer frequently scores a customer's credit rating based on a standard that lacks objectivity and requires considerable human resources to apply. Therefore, we recommend devising a credit risk assessment model by analyzing a mass volume of data or detecting concealed purchasing models, subsequently reducing the defaulted loan burden of small financial institutions. A database that integrates customer data can be established, to which highly effective data mining approaches are applied to identify the attributes of each customer account, such as overdraft records, outstanding loans and income. Credit ranking criteria based on a decision tree can then be established for all customers in the bank's database. In addition to greatly facilitating the decision of a banking officer regarding whether to grant a loan, the credit risk assessment model can reduce operating costs by enhancing the process flow. Moreover, the proposed model can pave the way for other potential data mining applications in financial institutions, such as more effective marketing strategies. The proposed model is also very promising for other industrial applications.

B

1. What will cause our company to lose its focus on product development and promotional strategies?

   the inability to interact compatibly with customers

2. What can be combined to construct an enhanced management model?

factors associated with customer relations and customer life cycle

3. What is the purpose of verifying and adjusting factors of the ranking module?

to ensure that a company continuously provides quality services

C

1. Why should we develop two forecasting models?

to estimate the demand of the elderly population in Taiwan for the available long-term healthcare resources

2. Why is forecasting the medical market trends (both in supply and demand) important?

It is a fundamental part of feasibility analysis.

3. Why is it possible to measure and forecast not only the quantity of early demand, but also the relationship between the demand and critical factors?

owing to the ability to accumulate a significant amount of data and identifying such factors

D

1. How do we recommend devising a credit risk assessment model?

by analyzing a mass volume of data or detecting concealed purchasing models

2. How are the attributes of each customer account identified?

by applying highly effective data mining approaches

3. How can the credit risk assessment model reduce operating costs?

by enhancing the process flow

E

1. How can one use this model in other business sectors?

2. What has seldom been adopted to forecast market trends in long-term care in

Taiwan?

3. What is the proposed model promising for?

F
Situation 1

1. B 2. A 3. C 4. B 5. B

Situation 2

1. B 2. C 3. B 4. A 5. C

Situation 3

1. B 2. B 3. C 4. A 5. C

G
Situation 1

1. B 2. B 3. A 4. C 5. A

Situation 2

2. C 2. B 3. B 4. A 5. A

Situation 3

1. A 2. B 3. C 4. B 5. A

I
Situation 4

According to the World Health Organization, Taiwan became an advanced aging society as of the end of 1993, with over 7% of its population 65 years or older. Aging in Taiwan explains the growing concern over the market demand for long-term care residential communities, in which middle-aged to senior individuals live independently in houses or apartment units designed for their special needs upon retirement. Many industries have already heavily invested in this emerging growth sector. However, although attempts have been made to evaluate the success of certain management practices in satisfying consumer demand in this growing market sector, few long-term care studies have attempted to identify success factors in managing residential communities of senior citizens. Therefore, we recommend developing an AHP-based method that enables administrators of senior citizen residential communities to identify critical factors for successful operations. A questionnaire survey can be designed to select the most appropriate sampling method. A valuation standard that reflects enterprise values can then be derived based on interviews with experts in the field. Next, critical factors for successful operations can be identified using the AHP method. The proposed AHP-based method can enable enterprises involved in the development of senior citizen residential communities to identify the features of and prerequisites for successful operations. The proposed method can enable administrators of residential communities of senior citizens to select the most feasible residential community during decision making by considering financial and market -related concerns to ensure the success of daily operations. In addition to enhancing the competency of administrators in making their residential communities efficient in this increasingly competitive sector, the proposed method can provide a valuable reference for experts, academics and investors.

Situation 5

Since its establishment in 1995, Taiwan's National Health Insurance scheme has strived to provide medical coverage for all of the island's residents under the auspices of the National Health Insurance Bureau. Despite the high quality of the medical care provided, hospitals often have difficulty in understanding customer's needs. More specifically, conventional statistical methods such as AHP and TOPSIS cannot analyze how patients select a hospital for treatment, making extremely difficult the establishment of effective business management strategies. Therefore, we recommend developing a patient selection model using AHP and TOPSIS, which analyzes incoming hospital patients in relation to public image of the hospital and the current market demand for specific services, ultimately gaining the confidence of patients in the quality of medical services.

A framing questionnaire can be designed based on the basic requirements of patients, including such intangible ones such as respect. The following criterion can be applied to analyze the questionnaire results: physicians must be qualified and reliable; medical staff must have received sufficient training; physicians must be willing to offer valuable clinical information; physicians must express concern for their patients; medical staff must display a professional attitude; and hospital administration must respect patient confidentiality. SPSS software can be used to analyze the results. Moreover, the following four assumptions are made. Public appraisal of the quality of medical treatment affects the overall results; the quality of service influences the expectations of hospital patients; patients' demands influence the quality of service, and a patient's experience influences the expected quality of service. The proposed patient selection model is established using AHP and TOPSIS, since conventional statistical models are useless. While influencing which hospital that a patient selects, the quality of hospital services does not necessarily improve customer satisfaction. Moreover, the proposed model helps hospitals develop an effective strategy for generating revenues independently of the national health insurance scheme.

Situation 6

Unforeseeable circumstances in the constantly fluctuating business climate require that enterprises adopt effective inventory management practices to improve their competitive edge.

Inventory stock is often regarded as a somewhat static resource with economic value, and the quality of its management directly affects company operations. Therefore, an effective stock inventory system is essential. However, while focusing on specific stock inventory systems, previous studies have seldom addressed the supply chain strategy for a stock inventory of multiple products with many suppliers. Either simulation or statistical approaches are adopted to establish inventory stock management policies. Simulation requires much time; it is therefore inefficient and yields questionable results. Statistical approaches offer guidelines aimed at simplifying either the inventory stock administration system or use of a complex system that is intended to establish approximate mathematical patterns; such approaches are often difficult to interpret. Therefore, we recommend the development of an inventory stock management model that coordinates the efforts of suppliers and retailers, and a model of distribution to minimize the total cost based on the metering method.

The (s, Q) policy that governs inventory stock and is determined between the supplier and the manufacturer can be used to reduce the minimum stock that must be carried, ultimately reducing the total associated with cost. Problems encountered by the supplier and the manufacturer in predicting the required amount of inventory stock can be addressed.

The stock model (s , Q) can be utilized to derive the inventory stock models of the supplier and manufacturer without complex mathematics. The supplier and the manufacturer can adopt the most appropriate control channel to determine the inventory stock cost, sales volume and orders in short supply. The proposed inventory management model can determine the most economic time to purchase and inventory stock policy for both the supplier and the manufacturer. By using random and the most appropriate control measures, the proposed management model can determine precisely the supplier and the manufacturers, reduce overhead costs and enable enterprise managers to select the most effective inventory stock policy.

J

1. Which success factors have few long-term care studies attempted to identify?
   those aimed at managing residential communities of senior citizens
2. Which aspects can enterprises involved in the development of senior citizen residential communities identify when using the proposed AHP-based method?
   the features of and prerequisites for successful operations
3. Which groups can the proposed method provide a valuable reference for?
   experts, academics and investors

K

1. What affects the overall results of the study?
   public appraisal of the quality of medical treatment
2. What influences the expectations of hospital patients?
   the quality of service
3. What factor influences which hospital that a patient selects but does not necessarily improve customer satisfaction?
   the quality of hospital services

L

1. Why are either simulation or statistical approaches adopted? to establish inventory stock management policies
2. Why is a model of distribution developed?
   to minimize the total cost based on the metering method
3. Why is the stock model (s , Q) utilized?

to derive the inventory stock models of the supplier and manufacturer without complex mathematics

M

1. Why can one design a questionnaire survey?
2. What cannot analyze how patients select a hospital for treatment?
3. How can one use the (s, Q) policy that governs inventory stock and is determined between the supplier and the manufacturer?

N

Situation 4

1. B   2. A   3. C   4. A   5. C

Situation 5

1. A   2. C   3. B   4. C   5. A

Situation 6

1. B   2. C   3. A   4. C   5. A

O

Situation 4

1. B   2. A   3. C   4. B   5. B

Situation 5

1. C   2. A   3. C   4. A   5. C

Situation 6

1. C   2. A   3. C   4. B   5. A

Answer Key
Persuasive Reports
說服力的展現

A

Situation 1

Many industrialized countries are affected by the globalization of the cosmetics sector. Taiwan's biotechnology industry has rapidly evolved in recent years, increasing marketing efforts in the local cosmetics sector, despite its having originally focused only on healthcare products.

For instance, according to the Industrial Technology Research Institute, revenues in the local cosmetics sector ranged between US$ 1.7 billion and US$ 1.8 billion in 2002. This figure contrasts with the US$ 7 hundred million revenue of the health food market and US$ 9 hundred million of the food testing market. Many female consumers regard cosmetics as a daily necessity, as reflected by the wide array of cosmetic brands in the marketplace. Given enormous female consumer demand and intense competition, manufacturers must better understand consumer purchasing behavior in this market niche.

Cosmetic manufacturers are concerned not only with marketing practices, but also with the potential lowering of product and service quality, necessitating the adoption of the 4P method. Although it has attracted considerable attention in the field of conventional marketing, the 4P method has seldom been explored with respect to its effectiveness in enhancing the competitiveness and market share of manufacturers of cosmetics. The failure of cosmetics manufacturers to adopt the 4P method in its marketing practices reduces market share of products and services. Accordingly, we have developed a novel 4P-based marketing strategy for the local cosmetics sector within Taiwan's biotech industry by considering consumer needs under the headings of product, price, promotion and place. This strategy enables managers in the cosmetics sector to understand consumer preferences better not only by learning how to identify and target potential customers efficiently, but also by establishing a retention strategy to maintain loyal customers and attract new ones.

A questionnaire is submitted to cosmetics manufacturers on the most appropriate marketing method, and then factor analysis is applied to the results based on adopts 4P principles. Adopting this 4P-based marketing strategy enables local cosmetic manufacturers to increase their share of the market in related products and services. The proposed strategy also helps planners to make decisions more objectively than is supported by conventional approaches, ultimately accelerating the effectiveness of the marketing process. In addition to encouraging product innovation, the 4P-based marketing strategy provides Taiwan's biotech industry with clear guidelines for equipping management in the local cosmetics sector with appropriate and efficient marketing policies that will ultimately reduce operating costs and enhance competitiveness. The proposed method also reveals how the biotechnology industry can incorporate 4P concepts to clarify the behavioral patterns of cosmetics customers.

We seek your prompt approval of the implementation of this novel marketing strategy in your organization so that you can more easily understand the behavioral patterns of your cosmetics customers.

Situation 2

Complex administrative procedures within Taiwan's National Health Insurance (NHI) scheme have led to errors in insurance claims and much inefficiency. For instance, adhering to all NHI regulations would require filling out more than 30 forms, depending on the task, such as submitting an insurance claim, adjusting a salary, and modifying the name of an insurer/claimant.

Errors made due to confusion over the forms cause NHI staff to spend much time in correcting errors and requesting insurers and claimants to amend erroneous information. Despite the enormous amount of administrative time and cost involved in handling such errors, the literature has not addressed the growing concern and larger implications of this situation. The inability to reduce slowly the amount of human resources involved in handling insurer and claimant errors and simplify administrative procedures as well as NHI forms, will lead to higher operational inefficiency. Such errors include those made on identification cards, such as regarding cardholder number, birthday or name. Sometimes the wrong form is completed. In practice, telephone, fax or mail is used to correct such errors, subsequently creating substantial overhead, and requiring additional time to be spent. Given the limited number of available NHI staff, simplifying forms and procedures is a priority.

We have developed a novel administrative procedure for classifying and simplifying forms for paying insurance premiums and filing other insurance-related claims under Taiwan's National Health Insurance (NHI) scheme. A database of detailed information on NHI insurance holders is accessed while ensuring the confidentiality of such information, reducing administrative costs and the number of personnel involved. Three insurance claim-related forms are developed to reduce the redundancy of the more than 30 existing forms, significantly reducing data processing. A highly restricted networked-based system is then accessed to ensure the confidentiality of NHI customer data and also reduce the amount of paperwork that insurance holders must submit. Accessing the system requires staff to set up an account and log in, and a systems administrator is assigned to maintain the smooth flow of operations. This smooth flow is especially important given the extremely heavy daily workload which requires staff to handle significant amounts of data daily, without time to maintain the system. The proposed administrative procedure streamlines the filing insurance-related claims by simplifying the forms and enabling efficient access to relevant customer data online. Importantly, the proposed procedure significantly reduces not only the amount of time required to fill out insurance claims, but also the postage fees. The network-based system accelerates data processing. This highly restricted networked-based system that ensures NHI customer confidentiality is unique in that it not only integrates the efforts of various organizations within the NHI scheme by providing data access, but also makes NHI administrative services more flexible for customers. We therefore strongly recommend that you adopt this administrative procedure to streamline the processing of insurance premiums and other insurance-related claims in Taiwan's National Health Insurance (NHI) scheme.

Situation 3

Although the Taiwanese government has been implementing separate frameworks for the medical and pharmaceutical sectors since 1997, the rate of filling of hospital prescription drugs by pharmacies is extremely low. This fact explains why over-the-counter drug purchases, along with sanitary and other related medical products, have become major revenue generators for pharmacies.

Local pharmacies have adopted a business model of one-stop shopping in recent years, allowing customers to purchase a wide range of medical and health food products. However, the inability to accurately forecast the share household consumption spent on medical and health care, or the number of local pharmacies to be established almost prevents managers from analyzing market competition accurately and developing effective strategies. To compensate for this limitation, we have devised a feasible forecasting method to estimate the growth of medical and health care expenditures as well as pharmaceutical units in Taiwan. Medical and health care expenditure data from 1999 to 2002 are obtained from the Budget Office of the Central Region, Department of Accounting and Statistics, Executive Yuan. Data on pharmaceutical units are obtained from the 2003 Annual Report of the Department of Health. Based on these data, the GM (1, N) model of the Grey theory is applied for forecasting purposes. The proposed forecasting method can accurately estimate medical and health care expenditures as well as the number of pharmacies to be established in Taiwan from 2008 to 2010. The proposed method can also identify how the share of household consumption on medical and health care is related to the number of pharmacies. Importantly, the proposed method provides a valuable reference for both governmental authorities in formulating policies and pharmaceutical managers in developing competitive marketing strategies. We therefore seek your authorization to adopt this forecasting method to ensure that an adequate number of pharmacies, located strategically, can meet health consumer demand in Taiwan.

B

1. Why must manufacturers better understand consumer purchasing behavior in the cosmetics sector?

   because of enormous female consumer demand and intense competition

2. Why does the 4P marketing strategy enable managers in the cosmetics sector to understand consumer preferences?

   because managers can not only learn how to identify and target potential customers efficiently, but also establish a retention strategy to maintain loyal customers and attract new ones

3. Why are local cosmetic manufacturers able to increase their share of the market in related products and services?

   because they can adopt this 4P-based marketing strategy

C

1. In what areas have complex administrative procedures within Taiwan's National Health Insurance (NHI) scheme led to errors?

in insurance claims and much inefficiency

2. What will lead to higher operational inefficiency?

the inability to reduce slowly the amount of human resources involved in handling insurer and claimant errors and simplify administrative procedures as well as NHI forms

3. What is unique about this highly restricted networked-based system that ensures NHI customer confidentiality?

It not only integrates the efforts of various organizations within the NHI scheme by providing data access, but also makes NHI administrative services more flexible for customers.

D

1. How can one explain why over-the-counter drug purchases, along with sanitary and other related medical products, have become major revenue generators for pharmacies?

because the rate of filling of hospital prescription drugs by pharmacies is extremely low

2. How does the proposed method provide a valuable reference for governmental authorities and pharmaceutical managers?

in formulating policies and developing competitive marketing strategies, respectively

3. How can one ensure that an adequate number of pharmacies, located strategically, can meet health consumer demand in Taiwan?

by adopting this forecasting method

E

1. Which organization reported that revenues in the local cosmetics sector ranged between US$ 1.7 billion and US$ 1.8 billion in 2002?

2. What has not addressed the growing concern and larger implications of the enormous amount of administrative time and cost involved in handling such errors?

3. How long has the Taiwanese government been implementing separate frameworks for the medical and pharmaceutical sectors?

F

Situation 1

1. A   2. C   3. B   4. C   5. A

Situation 2

1. B   2. A   3. B   4. A   5. C

Situation 3

1. C   2. B   3. B   4. A   5. C

G

Situation 1

1. B   2. B   3. A   4. A   5. B

Situation 2

1. B   2. A   3. C   4. A   5. C

Situation 3

1. C   2. C   3. B   4. B   5. C

I

Situation 4

The extremely competitive medical market sector in Taiwan and budget deficits associated with the island's National Health Insurance scheme have led to the implementation of a Global Budget System. Although hospitals highly prioritize attracting new patients, the patient turnover rate has received increasing attention. Hospitals must budget deficits retaining current patients and reduce the turnover rate of those going to other medical centers for treatment. Incapable of determining patient turnover rates precisely, hospitals face considerable expenditure in attracting new patients. The subsidies from the National Health Insurance scheme are declining, ultimately lowering the competitiveness of hospitals. Based on the above, we have developed a novel model to predict the turnover rate of customers in the medical sector. More specifically, the proposed model incorporates a novel set of management strategies that emphasize customer retention within the medical sector to increase a hospital's competitiveness.

A database of pertinent hospital patient data is exploited using a data mining method to identify the factors associated with customer turnover rate. A data mining approach that incorporates various data analysis tools is also adopted to discover interesting trends and relationships among various data sets. Pertinent literature is then reviewed to confirm the reliability of variables in the database. Next, questionnaires are sent to hospital administrators regarding customer satisfaction. Additionally, distinct consumer groups are identified. Cluster analysis is performed to distinguish among all consumer groups. Neural networks are used to enhance the model accuracy, and the results are subsequently analyzed. In addition to providing the medical sector with more accurate guidelines on patient retention and marketing, the proposed model greatly helps hospitals to provide high-quality and flexible health care services that will ultimately enhance their public image by markedly improving relations with patients. Apart from identifying the major factors underlying customer turnover rate, the proposed model can also offer feasible strategies to cope with this dilemma and achieve management goals. Furthermore, the proposed model can contribute to efforts to maintain customers in the highly competitive medical market sector and provide a valuable reference for healthcare managers in enhancing customer relations. We seek your approval to adopt this customer retention strategy that can ultimately reduce the operating costs of hospitals and increase the total number of patients.

Situation 5

With an increasingly elderly population, Taiwan must effectively address the increasing demand for long-term healthcare facilities and services. The potential growth of this non-profit market sector, the largest in Taiwan, is immense, and healthcare providers cannot resist expanding into this area. Therefore, forecasting (both supply and demand) trends in the long-term care market is a fundamental part of feasibility analysis. Both governmental policymakers of social welfare trends and commercial investors rely strongly on forecasts to remain abreast of regulations that govern health finance policies and to develop new inventory projects.

Although modeling methods have seldom been adopted to forecast trends in the long-term care market in Taiwan, most studies have focused on expert conjecture or previous sector growth to forecast market supply and demand. Those methods not only neglect the market and factors that govern the long-term healthcare sector, but also result in individual and organizational estimates of demand with high variance. Therefore, we have developed two forecasting models to estimate the market demand of the elderly population of Taiwan on available resources in the long-term healthcare sector. A multi-regression model is developed to measure and forecast not only the elderly population in Taiwan, but also the relationship between the elderly population variation and critical factors.

Following the submission of a questionnaire to institutional managers as well as public and private sector investors, critical factors associated with further development of Taiwan's long-term healthcare sector are identified from the replies with reference to pertinent research. A GM (1, 1) model based on the Grey Theory is then developed to forecast accurately the supply of Taiwan's long term care facilities and services using data obtained from the Ministry of Interior's website. In addition to identifying factors that affect the elderly population, the proposed forecasting models measure precisely the demand for and supply of long-term healthcare resources in Taiwan. Moreover, the proposed models not only are a valuable resource for institutional managers, private sector investors and academics, but also support a feasible health care policy strategy to meet the demand of this rapidly growing sector. We strongly recommend that your healthcare organization adopt these forecasting methods not only to determine the accuracy of forecasting reports, but also to determine what policies or inventory projects to implement.

Situation 6

Lending and investing are common business practices of financial organizations. Most Taiwanese enterprises are small- and medium-sized, explaining why their credit rating status is often unknown. Banks have thus expended considerable time and human resources in diagnosing the ability of enterprises to repay loans, to reduce non-performing loans (NPLs). Further exacerbation of the NPL crisis would cause a shortage of operating funds in banks, ultimately harming investor interests, stockholder profits and institutional reputations. Banks loan to, or invest in, organizations based on whether they have a good credit rating, which is determined by investigations made by financial experts into financial reports to determine current status and credit classification. Such time-consuming and prohibitively expensive investigations do not always yield satisfactory results and even miss market opportunities. The inability of loaning institutions to estimate accurately the credit rating of enterprises leads to misclassifications that result in inestimable losses. Machine learning methods cannot increase the accuracy of expert systems owing to the inability to accurately predict credit ratings. To solve this problem, we have developed a novel classification model for small- and medium-sized enterprises, capable of increasing the accuracy of classification of credit ratings of enterprises and reducing administrative expense.

Data from small- and medium-sized enterprises are accumulated and categorized. They are processed using a fuzzy set to store additional information. Fuzzy data are then clustered using a two-stage clustering approach to classify credit ratings properly.

An ANN structure is constructed. Additionally, the accuracy of the ANN classification machine is estimated with ten-fold cross validation to identify the most efficient machine. Moreover, results obtained from the above tests are tabulated and compared with those in the literature to verify data authenticity. The proposed classification model increases predictive accuracy from 10% (as achieved by the conventional classification system) to 80%, subsequently reducing operating costs significantly. In addition to increasing the efficiency of obtaining data from small- and medium-sized enterprises, and reducing operational costs during estimation, the proposed model provides important guidelines for banks. We therefore highly recommend that your institution adopt this novel classification model to increase your accuracy in classifying the credit ratings of lending enterprises and significantly lower administrative expenses.

J

1. Why is the competitiveness of hospitals ultimately lowered?

   because the subsidies from the National Health Insurance scheme are declining.

2. Why is a data mining approach adopted that incorporates various data analysis tools?

to discover interesting trends and relationships among various data sets

3. Why can this customer retention strategy ultimately reduce the operating costs of hospitals and increase the total number of patients?

because it can contribute to efforts to maintain customers in the highly competitive medical market sector and provide a valuable reference for healthcare managers in enhancing customer relations

K

1. What regulations must governmental policymakers of social welfare trends and commercial investors abreast of?

those that govern health finance policies and to develop new inventory projects

2. What have most studies on the long-term care market in Taiwan focused on?

expert conjecture or previous sector growth to forecast market supply and demand

3. What can adoption of these forecasting methods determine?

the accuracy of forecasting reports and what policies or inventory projects to implement

L

1. How could investor interests, stockholder profits and institutional reputations be ultimately harmed?

by further exacerbation of the NPL crisis that would cause a shortage of operating funds in banks

2. How is the current status and credit classification of borrowing organizations determined?

by investigations made by financial experts into financial reports

3. How could misclassifications that result in inestimable losses occur?

the inability of loaning institutions to estimate accurately the credit rating of enterprises

M

1. What does the novel set of management strategies in the proposed model emphasize?

2. Where is data obtained to forecast accurately the supply of Taiwan's long term care facilities and services?

3. What are common business practices of financial organizations?

N

Situation 4

1. C   2. B   3. A   4. C   5. A

Situation 5

1. B   2. B   3. C   4. A   5. A

Situation 6

1. B   2. C   3. B   4. A   5. B

O

Situation 4

1. A   2. C   3. A   4. C   5. B

Situation 5

1. A   2. C   3. A   4. C   5. B

Situation 6

1. A   2. A   3. B   4. C   5. B

Answer Key
Informal Technical Reports
非正式實用工程技術報告

A
Situation 1

Our project addressed how to identify major success factors of the pharmaceutical sector in Taiwan for purposes of devising more effective customer-based strategies. The Taiwanese government has relaxed restrictions on the domestic medical sector in recent years, enabling consumers to purchase over-the-counter drugs, vitamins and other medicines in supermarkets or through mass merchandisers. Consequently, the profits of local pharmacies have been negatively affected. Although pharmacies have attempted to strengthen consumer demand through one-stop shopping, such as by selling sanitary and other related medical products, overall revenues have not significantly increased. Therefore, we developed a model based on key successful factors (KSF) that incorporates consumer purchasing factors on various hierarchical levels to enable local pharmacies in Taiwan to reform their marketing strategies. A questionnaire based on consumer purchasing factors identified from pertinent literature was sent to consumers and pharmaceutical managers. Major consumer purchasing factors were then analyzed and ranked using the analytic hierarchical process. The proposed KSF model enables pharmaceutical managers to execute business operations more effectively by allowing them to modify marketing strategies based on inconsistencies between consumer demand and the response to that demands. Importantly, the proposed model can be applied to other retail stores, enhancing their business operations.

Situation 2

We recently attempted to determine how to measure accurately the customer turnover rate in our hospital. The extremely competitive medical market sector in Taiwan and budget deficits associated with the island's National Health

Insurance scheme have led to the implementation of a Global Budget System. Although hospitals heavily prioritize attracting new patients, the patient turnover rate has received increasing attention. Relatively few studies have addressed this aspect of the medical sector, and most have used conventional approaches to calculate the number of patients on a daily basis without differentiating between new and return patients. Therefore, we developed a novel predictive model of the turnover rate of customers in the medical sector to determine how to retain them. A database of pertinent hospital patient data was utilized and data mining used to identify the factors associated with the customer turnover rate. Pertinent literature was then reviewed to confirm the reliability of variables in the database. Next, questionnaires were sent to hospital administrators regarding customer satisfaction, and the results were subsequently analyzed. The proposed predictive model can be adopted to design and implement precautionary measures to reduce customer turnover rates. In addition to identifying the major factors that govern customer turnover rate, the proposed model offers feasible strategies for overcoming this issue and achieving management goals. Moreover, the proposed model contributes to efforts to maintain customers in the highly competitive medical market sector and provides a valuable reference for healthcare managers in enhancing customer relations.

Situation 3

Our group has thoroughly explored the difficulty of forecasting the supply of and demand for long-term healthcare in Taiwan. Although Taiwan's growing elderly population has increased the demand for institutional-based health care, the institutional health care sector obviously varies greatly island wide in the level and quality of services and facilities, resulting in significant public concern. Concern over the correlation between quality of institutional care and working capital has seldom been addressed, and most studies have focused on legislation, human resource management and approaches to enhancing patient care. Therefore, we analyzed the effect of various operating costs on the quality of institutional healthcare. Exactly how the quality and operating costs of institutional healthcare correlate with each other was analyzed using financial statements and customer satisfaction indexes. Relevant non-digitized data was then calculated using a gray system-based mathematical method and fuzzy theory. After the fuzzy theory had been applied to digitize the data, the gray system was used to rank and verify the importance of various operating costs and the quality of institutional healthcare. The results of this study enable institutional healthcare facility managers not only to strengthen areas of corporate management, but also to provide high-quality long-term healthcare.

B

1. Why have the profits of local pharmacies been negatively affected?
   because consumers can purchase over-the-counter drugs, vitamins and other medicines in supermarkets or through mass merchandisers
2. Why did we develop a model based on key successful factors (KSF) that incorporates consumer purchasing factors on various hierarchical levels?
   to enable local pharmacies in Taiwan to reform their marketing strategies
3. Why are pharmaceutical managers able to modify marketing strategies based on inconsistencies between consumer demand and the response to that demands?
   because the proposed KSF model enables pharmaceutical managers to execute business operations more effectively

C

1. What has received increasing attention?
   the patient turnover rate

2. What was reviewed to confirm the reliability of variables in the database?

pertinent literature

3. What does the proposed model contribute to?

efforts to maintain customers in the highly competitive medical market sector

D

1. How have most long-term health care studies been conducted?

by focusing on legislation, human resource management and approaches to enhancing patient care

2. How was the correlation between the quality and operating costs of institutional healthcare analyzed?

by using financial statements and customer satisfaction indexes

3. How will the results of this study help institutional healthcare facility managers?

to strengthen areas of corporate management and provide high-quality long-term healthcare

E

1. How were major consumer purchasing factors analyzed and ranked?

2. How can one adopt the proposed predictive model?

3. What has increased the demand for institutional-based health care?

F

Situation 1

1. C   2. B   3. B   4. C   5. B

Situation 2

1. C   2. B   3. A   4. C   5. B

Answer Key
Informal Technical Reports
非正式實用工程技術報告

Situation 3

1. C   2. A   3. A   4. C   5. C

G

Situation 1

1. C   2. B   3. A   4. C   5. B

Situation 2

1. A   2. B   3. C   4. A   5. A

Situation 3

1. B   2. B   3. C   4. A   5. A

I

Situation 4

The bank's Board of Directors expressed concern over how to identify, acquire and retain loyal and profitable customers by more effectively managing customer relations. Both the increasing popularity of card use and the growing number of Internet-based promotional activities in Taiwan have enabled banking institutions to obtain extensive customer data. In addition to helping banking institutions efficiently execute customer management and service management, thoroughly analyzing such data can optimize marketing management practices. Corporate survival in the future hinges on the ability to know and treat customers well based on analyses of pertinent data. Therefore, our research group developed a customer ranking model that can analyze the dynamic purchasing behavior of customers and identify those who can potentially generate bank revenues. Those behavioral results were used to devise diverse promotional strategies or customize products or services according to consumer needs, thus achieving market differentiation and effective management of customer relations. Using the proposed model, factors of the ranking module were verified and adjusted to ensure that a company continuously provides quality services. The proposed customer ranking model can be adopted to manage effectively customer relations, significantly reducing promotional costs and allowing sales staff to concentrate on identifying potential customers. The customer's value can be determined and this model significantly enhances the ability to attract new customers. Furthermore, it can be used in other business sectors to enhance the ability to identify, acquire and retain loyal and profitable customers.

Situation 5

We recently addressed how our hospital's public relations department can implement marketing practices to increase our competitiveness in the medical sector. Governmental policy over Taiwan's National Health Insurance (NHI) scheme continuously changes, especially in light of increasing medical costs and premiums as well as concern over the potential lowering of the quality of health care that is offered. Hospitals must thus emphasize marketing practices that attract patients through public relations. Although the role of public relations in business marketing has received considerable attention, its role in hospital marketing has seldom been addressed. Therefore, we launched a marketing strategy for our hospital that emphasizes identifying and satisfying the needs of a patient. Factor analysis of a customer's needs was performed by conducting personal interviews. The results were then analyzed, and vital factors identified. The proposed marketing strategy increases customer satisfaction by over 10% through hospital marketing, by significantly reducing overhead and work time. The proposed marketing strategy provides a valuable reference for hospital managers to develop an optimization procedure for marketing practices.

Answer Key
Informal Technical Reports
非正式實用工程技術報告

Situation 6

Our recent project addressed how to select the optimal location and size of Taiwanese correctional facilities, thus minimizing societal risks. Given the stagnant Taiwanese economy and increasing unemployment in recent years, growing crime rates and subsequent convictions have led to a high prisoner population. However, the conventional means of selecting the locations of correctional facilities is not objective, but often depends on the subjective judgment of decision makers. Therefore, we attempted to identify factors that affect the infrastructure and safety of correctional facilities in Taiwan by using the analytic hierarchy process (AHP) to determine the optimal target population and location of such facilities. Location-related factors were identified through an exhaustive literature review and consultation with experts in the field. Exactly how these individual factors are related to each other was also determined using AHP. Next, a questionnaire was submitted to administrators of correctional facilities to elucidate the correct factors. Additionally, all factors involved in selecting the target population and location of correctional facilities were analyzed using AHP. Based on those factors, the optimal location was chosen. The optimal target population and location of future correctional facilities are determined from the analysis results. The concerns of residents near a newly established correctional facility can be alleviated by reassuring them of the security features and pointing out the potential economic benefits of the facility. While correctional facilities operate under a governmental budget, the optimal location can reduce the cost of facility operations and maintenance-related management. The results of this study provide a valuable reference for governmental authorities in selecting the optimal location and size of correctional facilities, minimizing societal risk. Furthermore, this optimal location strategy encourages other law enforcement organizations to understand how location planning can ensure the security of an inmate population, reduce societal risks and alleviate public concern by making local residents aware of the potential benefits of such facilities.

J

1. How can banking institutions optimize marketing management practices?

   by thoroughly analyzing customer management and service management-related data

2. How can one ensure corporate survival in the future?

   by knowing and treating customers well based on analyses of pertinent data

3. How can one significantly reduce promotional costs and allow sales staff to concentrate on identifying potential customers?

   by adopting the proposed customer ranking model to manage effectively customer relations

K

1. What marketing practices must hospitals emphasize?

   those that attract patients through public relations

2. What has previous research seldom addressed?

   the role of public relations in hospital marketing

3. By what percentage can the proposed marketing strategy increase customer satisfaction?

   by over 10%

L

1. Why does the conventional means of selecting the locations of correctional facilities lack objectivity?

   It often depends on the subjective judgment of decision makers.

2. Why was it possible to alleviate the concerns of residents near a newly established correctional facility?

by reassuring them of the security features and pointing out the potential economic benefits of the facility

3. Why are law enforcement organizations that adopt this optimal location strategy able to alleviate public concern?

by making local residents aware of the potential benefits of such facilities

M

1. How can one achieve market differentiation and effective management of customer relations?

2. How does the proposed marketing strategy provide a valuable reference for hospital managers?

3. How were location-related factors identified?

N
Situation 4
1. C   2. A   3. B   4. C   5. B
Situation 5
1. B   2. C   3. C   4. B   5. A
Situation 6
1. A   2. C   3. B   4. A   5. B

O
Situation 4
1. C   2. B   3. C   4. A   5. C

Situation 5

1. B   2. B   3. C   4. A   5. C

Situation 6

1. A   2. C   3. C   4. A   5. B

Answer Key
Employment Application Letters
求職申請信函

A

Situation 1

In response to your recent advertisement in the September edition of <u>Hospital Administrator Magazine</u> for the research position of a radiotechnologist, I feel that my strong academic background and practical experiences make me highly qualified for this position.

I received a Bachelor's degree in Chemical Engineering from National Taipei University, where the departmental curriculum sparked my interest in various directions. I became especially interested in medical imagery and radiotherapy of tumors, particularly for curative purposes. Several years of academic study have left me with the deep impression that study is not just for securing employment. As indicated in the attached resume, my recent completion of a Master's degree in Medical Imagery attests to my commitment to pursuing a research career. While attempting to understand the nature of the tumor in a patient, I focused my graduate study on the role of radiotherapy in eradication. The results of my research have already contributed to efforts to treat patients with tumors more effectively. Specifically, I am interested in how radiation therapy of tumors can facilitate patient recovery - an area of research that has received increasing attention in recent years. Working in your hospital would hopefully allow me not only to pursue some of my above research interests, but also to contribute to the overall welfare of those patients who are seeking therapeutic treatment.

Your hospital offers comprehensive and challenging training for those undertaking research in radiation therapy and protection. Such training could provide me a marvelous opportunity to put my above knowledge and expertise into practice. If employed at your hospital, I will apply my professional knowledge of how to estimate the optimum dosage level for tumor patients efficiently and accurately. My professional knowledge will directly facilitate the recovery of tumor patients undergoing therapy. I am confident that my solid academic background in radiological technology will prove to be an invaluable asset to your hospital. I look forward to meeting with you in person to discuss this position further.

Yours truly,

Mary Li

Situation 2

The position of a pharmaceutical sales representative that you recently advertised in the February 5, 2007 edition of <u>The China Times</u> closely matches my career direction and previous academic training.

Commercial development planning has enthralled me since I took part in a business management training course sponsored by the Council of Labor Affairs. I also focused on development planning in the medical sector while studying in the Department of Healthcare Management at Yuanpei University and later for a Masters in Business Management from the same university. As you can see in the attached resume, while pursuing a graduate degree, I learned of advanced theories in my field and acquired practical training to enhance my ability to identify and resolve problems efficiently. Moreover, closely studying business practices in the medical sector at undergraduate and graduate school has equipped me with the competence to contribute to the development of management strategies to resolve unforeseeable problems efficiently, hopefully at your company.

I am even more confident that I can significantly contribute to your franchise. While offering famous medical product brands from the United States in the Taiwan market, your franchise prioritizes quality and the work professionals in a diverse range of medical fields. Specifically, I hope to contribute to your marketing efforts, logistics management and medical research in areas that are likely to grow in the future.

As a community pharmacy chain, your franchiser has distinguished itself in overcoming operational difficulties and maintaining good discipline to manage its business units effectively. I firmly believe that if I successful in securing employment at your company, my strong academic and practical knowledge, curricular and otherwise, will enable me to contribute positively to your corporation. In summary, my marketing research and excellent analytical capabilities will support your company's commitment to offering quality products and services.

I will contact you shortly by telephone with the hope of scheduling an interview.

Yours truly,

John Chuang

Situation 3

I would like to apply for the marketing position in the information technology sector that you advertised recently in the March issue of Information Today. Your company would provide me with an excellent environment not only to realize fully my career aspirations, but also to apply theoretical knowledge management concepts taught in graduate school in a practical work setting.

In addition to my strong interest in information technology, I have acquired many valuable research experiences through graduate studies in Business Management at National Taiwan Ocean University. These two ingredients are definitely crucial to my fully realizing my career aspirations. I will be able further to refine my skills if employed at your company. My logical competence and analytical skills reached new heights during two years of intensive graduate level training.

As detailed in the attached resume, related project experiences have greatly strengthened my independent research capabilities and statistical as well as analytical skills. Your company offers a competitive work environment for highly skilled professionals: these ingredients are essential to my continually improving my knowledge, skills and expertise in the above area.

As a leader in the information technology sector, your company is renowned for its state-of-the-art products and services, as well as outstanding product research and technical capabilities. As I hope to become a member of your corporate family, the particular expertise developed in graduate school and my strong academic and practical knowledge skills will definitely make me an asset to any collaborative product development effort. Offering more than just my technical expertise, I am especially interested in how your company's marketing and related management departments reach strategic decisions. Employment at your company will undoubtedly expose me to new fields as long as I remain open and do not restrict myself to the range of my previous academic training.

In sum, my ability to excel in information technology proved especially effective in devising marketing strategies for research purposes. Despite lacking knowledge of a particular topic at the outset, I quickly absorb new information and adapt to new situations. I believe that your company will find this a highly desired quality. Please contact me at your earliest convenience to schedule an interview.

Yours truly,
Julie Yeh

B

1. Why does the attached resume attest to Mary's commitment to pursuing a research career?

her recent completion of a Master's degree in Medical Imagery

2. Why is Mary's interest in how radiation therapy of tumors can facilitate patient recovery an important one?

because it is an area of research that has received increasing attention in recent years

3. Why is Mary confident that she will be an invaluable asset to the hospital?

because of her solid academic background in radiological technology

C

1. What enhanced John's ability to identify and resolve problems efficiently while in graduate school?

his learning of advanced theories in his field and acquired practical training

2. What equipped John with the competence to contribute to the development of management strategies to resolve unforeseeable problems efficiently?

his close study of business practices in the medical sector at undergraduate and graduate school

3. What will support the company's commitment to offering quality products and services?

John's marketing research and excellent analytical capabilities

D

1. Where was Julie taught theoretical knowledge management concepts?

in graduate school

2. Where are Julie's related project experiences detailed?

in the attached resume

3. Where would Julie gain exposure to new fields as long as she remains open and does not restrict herself to the range of her previous academic training?

at the company that she is applying to for employment

E

1. What month's edition of Hospital Administrator Magazine advertised for the research position of a radiotechnologist?

2. When did John learn of advanced theories in his field and acquire practical training?

3. When did Julie's logical competence and analytical skills reach new heights?

F

Situation 1

1. C   2. C   3. B   4. A   5. B

Situation 2

1. B   2. A   3. A   4. C   5. C

Situation 3

1. C   2. A   3. B   4. C   5. B

G

Situation 1

1. B   2. C   3. A   4. A   5. C

Situation 2

1. A   2. C   3. C   4. B   5. A

Situation 3

1. A   2. A   3. C   4. A   5. B

I

Situation 4

Answer Key
Employment Application Letters
求職申請信函

From a recent March 15th posting on the Nursing Today website, I learned that your hospital is recruiting for a supervisor in the emergency care department. Fully understanding that your hospital hopes to operate an emergency care department that can coordinate its efforts with an emergency medical network in Taipei, I am confident of my ability to handle required administrative tasks, especially in light of my solid nursing experience and management skills.

From my early nursing experience to my current work as a professional nurse in an emergency care department, I have been involved in many efforts that require critical patient care. They have included responding to the devastating Chi Chi earthquake that hit Taiwan on September 21, 2000, setting up a medical station at San Xia Da Bao River, and counteracting the deadly SARS virus in our hospital environment. While my job often requires me to respond to many unforeseeable circumstances, I remain fascinated by the dynamics of my profession, and enjoy a deep sense of satisfaction when helping others.

Renowned for its efforts to remain abreast of governmental strategies and current trends, your hospital will establish a second medical center in Taipei County in the near future. I am most impressed that this new center will provide high-quality medical treatment to more critical patients in a relatively short time. With my decade of experience in emergency care departments and graduate degree in Business Management, I believe that I can significantly contribute to efforts to train emergency care professionals and assess the process and preparation of emergency medical staff.

Given my experience, I will definitely be able to contribute to your hospital's efforts to satisfy the demands of medical consumers while effectively controlling overhead. In addition to my background in the nursing profession, I strive constantly to integrate my substantial management experiences with theoretical knowledge, making me more adept in making the correct strategic decisions in our hospital's emergency medical unit. I am confident of my ability to contribute significantly to your efforts to elevate the quality of healthcare management if given the opportunity to work in your organization. The attached resume includes my contact details. Please give me this opportunity.

Yours truly,

Sally Huang

Situation 5

I would like to apply for the managerial position posted recently on your healthcare organization's website. Abundant experience of administrative work while in the military, and extracurricular activities in the student association at university, will definitely help me become oriented with my new responsibilities at your company. My familiarity with several analytic methods in decision science, gained during graduate school, is another strong asset that I bring to your company. I can apply such methods more flexibly after securing employment in a non-profit organization such as yours. Moreover, my previous academic and work experience will enable me to explain results of analyses more clearly to enable the organization to reach management decisions efficiently.

As indicated in the attached resume, my graduate degree in Business Administration at National Central University offered specialized curricula that not only strengthened my knowledge of modern business practices and English writing skills to publish my research findings, but also equipped me with the necessary skills to contribute significantly to the workplace. My diverse academic interests and strong curricular training reflect my ability not only to see beyond the conventional limits of a discipline and fully comprehend how the field relates to other fields, but also to apply strong analytical and problem-solving skills.

As a renowned leader in the long-term healthcare sector, your company has impressive organizational objectives, combined with a strong management structure and diversity of training courses. This strong organizational commitment is reflected in the high quality services that you provide to your customers. As a member of your corporation, I hope to participate actively in your company's external affairs. My work experience and solid academic background will enable me to comprehend and familiarize myself with all of the commercial practices of your healthcare organization in a relatively short time.

In addition to a solid academic background, a good manager should have strong communicative, organizational and management skills. I am confident that I possess them. I look forward to meeting with you in person to discuss in detail what this position encompasses.

Yours truly,

Jason Tong

Situation 6

Regarding the information management position advertised recently in the December issue of Information Today, I am a competent candidate. My project management experience has enabled me to deal carefully with others and resolve disputes efficiently. My love of challenges will enable me to satisfy constantly fluctuating customer requirements in information integration projects, hopefully at your company.

Having devoted myself to developing information systems in the semiconductor industry for over a decade, I have developed a particular interest in enhancing work productivity using the latest information technologies. I have also spent considerable time in researching system integration for manufacturing applications on UNIX-based systems. As shown in the accompanying resume, critical thinking skills developed during undergraduate and graduate training have enabled me not only to explore beyond the surface of manufacturing-related issues and delve into their underlying implications, but also to conceptualize problems in different ways. While participating in several MOSEL group projects, I also learned how to address supply chain-related issues to broaden my perspective of potential applications of finance and decision making; these areas are now my main focus.

Renowned for effectively dealing with unforeseeable emergencies and enhancing customer services, your company has established a vision that deeply impresses me. Moreover, I am attracted to your company's advanced financial information system for analyzing business transactions models, a system which will equip me with the competence to contribute more significantly to your organization's excellence in marketing. If I am successful in gaining employment in your company, both my solid academic training and my research on information system development will make me a strong asset in your efforts to upgrade e-business operations, such as online queries, payments and account transferals.

I am confident that my work experience in software development has equipped me with the necessary competence to address effectively information technology-related problems in your company. Please contact me at your earliest convenience to schedule an interview.

Yours truly,

Scott Liao

J

1. How does Sally's solid nursing experience and management skills make her feel?

   confident of her ability to handle required administrative tasks

2. How does Sally enjoy a deep sense of satisfaction?

   when helping others

3. How is Sally qualified to significantly contribute to efforts to train emergency care professionals and assess the process and preparation of emergency medical staff?

   her decade of experience in emergency care departments and graduate degree in Business Management

K

1. What will enable Jason to explain results of analyses more clearly to enable the organization to reach management decisions efficiently?

   his previous academic and work experience

2. What enables Jason to see beyond the conventional limits of a discipline and fully comprehend how the field relates to other fields?

   his diverse academic interests and strong curricular training

3. What will enable Jason to comprehend and familiarize himself with all of the commercial practices of the healthcare organization in a relatively short time?

   his work experience and solid academic background

L

1. Why has Scott devoted over a decade to developing information systems in the semiconductor industry for over a decade?

   to enhance work productivity using the latest information technologies

2. Why has Scott spent considerable time in researching system integration?

for manufacturing applications on UNIX-based systems

3. Why did Scott learn how to address supply chain-related issues?

to broaden his perspective of potential applications of finance and decision making

M

1. How long has Sally been involved in many efforts that require critical patient care?

2. How is the company's strong organizational commitment reflected?

3. What have Scott to explore beyond the surface of manufacturing-related issues and delve into their underlying implications?

N

Situation 4

1. B   2. A   3. C   4. A   5. A

Situation 5

1. C   2. A   3. C   4. B   5. B

Situation 6

1. B   2. C   3. A   4. B   5. A

O

Situation 4

1. A   2. B   3. C   4. A

Situation 5

1. A   2. C   3. B   4. C   5. B

Situation 6

Answer Key
Training Application Letters
訓練申請信函

1. C   2. B   3. C   4. A   5. B

A
Situation 1

To build upon my academic and professional experience, I would like to serve as a self-supported guest researcher in the oncology department of your hospital for a three-month period, hopefully during my upcoming summer vacation.

The attached resume and recommendation letters provide further details of my solid academic background and professional experiences. As a graduate student of Medical Imagery at Yuanpei University, I actively participated in a project aimed at identifying prognostic factors of breast cancer and subsequently developing an effective prognostic method to increase the survival rate of breast cancer patients. The identified prognostic factors provide a valuable reference for radiologists in devising a therapeutic treatment program for patients. The prognostic factors, identified in that research effort, can also benefit the cancer patients in your hospital, an organization that already has an excellent reputation in the medical field and has gained international recognition for its own research advances.

The variety of research projects and departments within your company committed to implementing them is quite impressive, explaining why you have taken a leading role in the medicine and pharmaceutical fields. Working at your company would definitely promote my professional development. Following my gaining medical imagery expertise in graduate school, I believe that my solid academic training and practical knowledge will contribute to your company's efforts to elevate its reputation and new technology capabilities, even during the short three-month period at your laboratory.

As for the details of this training practicum, identifying adequate therapeutic treatment and prognostic factors is essential in radiology technology - a field in whose managerial aspects I am very interested. As for my professional interests, I have always been interested in identifying prognostic factors of breast cancer or, more specifically, those factors that can elevate the curative rate for patients during treatment. In this area of research, the potential technical and medical sector opportunities appear to be limitless. Please let me know if you require additional materials. I look forward to your favorable reply.

Yours truly,

John Li

Situation 2

My academic advisor, Dr. Cheng, recommended that I contact you regarding the possibility of a guest researcher stay in your laboratory, hopefully for a six-month period under your direct supervision. Despite my strong academic background and numerous work experiences, I hope to gain further training at your hospital owing to its commitment to excellent medical image processing as well as advanced PACS instrumentation. In addition to improving my technical expertise, I am also interested in enhancing my management proficiency within your organization.

My interest in medicine and physics, since my childhood, has led to my successful completion of both a Bachelor's degree in Radiology Technology and a Master's degree in Medical Imagery from National Tsing Hua University. Since then, I have been working as a radiology technician in the radiology department of a hospital, which combines digital technologies and the Internet. Undergraduate and graduate level courses in radiochemistry in the medical imagery field instilled in me a wide array of theoretical concepts related to radiopharmaceutical synthesis. My graduate school research often involved deriving complex radiopharmaceutical synthesis models and modifying radiopharmaceutical practices in nuclear medicine to meet my research needs. I have also attended several international conferences on radiology technology, further widening my exposure to the radiochemistry profession.

Through this training opportunity in your laboratory, your highly skilled professionals would provide me with an excellent research environment, advanced equipment and related resources to enhance my research capabilities so that I can thrive in this dynamic profession. With a long tradition of commitment, your hospital offers extensive training courses for technical staff in all hospital departments to maintain competitiveness. Working in your organization, even for a short time, would definitely benefit my professional development.

As for details of this guest internship, your department offers state-of-the-art instrumentation and clinical training of those involved in researching PET/CT-related topics. Such exposure would definitely further my knowledge skills. I look forward to your thoughts regarding this proposed residency.

Yours truly,

Mary Chang

Situation 3

Eager to strengthen my expertise in optimizing the results obtained from the picture archiving communication system (PACS) at our hospital's Medical Imagery Department, I hope to serve in your laboratory as a self-supported guest worker for six months to compensate for my lack of training in this area. As a leader in the medical field, your hospital would provide me with many collaborative opportunities not only to provide better medical care for patients through your solid training, but also to improve my expertise continually.

As I recently completed my Master's degree in Medical Imagery, graduate school has oriented me about how to integrate diagnostic programs with the Internet and related technologies, greatly improving a patient's outcome. Graduate school also enabled me not only to grasp the clinical implications of different diagnostic tests, but also to operate medical instrumentation appropriately. These skills help me to ensure that a patient receives an accurate diagnosis.

As evidenced by your highly respected training courses on nuclear medicine, your hospital possesses state-of-the-art equipment and expertise in handling stroke patients. For instance, your excellent staff has perfected the skill of easily distinguishing ischemia from hemorrhaging. If granted this research opportunity, I would bring to your organization a solid academic background and practical expertise that can hopefully contribute to your ongoing efforts. Moreover, having passed an extremely difficult entrance examination for medical professionals in this field, I believe that my expertise of imagery medicine will be an asset to any clinical department to which I belong.

During this training opportunity, I will be especially interested in how medical images facilitate the diagnosis and treatment of diseases. In particular, computers with valuable medical software can provide clinical physicians with data that can help determine the course of medical care. Training at your hospital would enable me to create precise anatomic images to confirm a specific malady. Let me know if you require materials in addition to the enclosed resume and recommendation letters. I look forward to your favorable reply.

Yours truly,

Answer Key
Training Application Letters
訓練申請信函

Lisa Yeh

B

1. Why do the identified prognostic factors provide a valuable reference for radiologists?

   to devise a therapeutic treatment program for patients

2. Why has the company that John is applying to taken a leading role in the medicine and pharmaceutical fields?

   because of the variety of research projects and departments that are committed to implementing them

3. Why has John always been interested in identifying prognostic factors of breast cancer?

   because those factors can elevate the curative rate for patients during treatment

C

1. What led to Mary's successful completion of both a Bachelor's degree in Radiology Technology and a Master's degree in Medical Imagery?

   her interest in medicine and physics since childhood

2. What instilled in Mary a wide array of theoretical concepts related to radiopharmaceutical synthesis?

   undergraduate and graduate level courses in radiochemistry in the medical imagery field

3. What did Mary's graduate school research often involve? deriving complex radiopharmaceutical synthesis models and modifying radiopharmaceutical practices in nuclear medicine

D

1. How could the many collaborative opportunities that the hospital provides benefit Lisa?

   by allowing her to provide better medical care for patients and to improve her expertise continually

2. How did the hospital's training courses on nuclear medicine become highly respected?

   owing to its state-of-the-art equipment and expertise in handling stroke patients

3. How does Lisa hope to contribute to the hospital's ongoing efforts?

   by bringing to the organization a solid academic background and practical expertise

E

1. How long does John want to serve as a self-supported guest researcher in the hospital's oncology department?

2. How could the laboratory's highly skilled professionals enhance Mary's research capabilities?

3. In what area did graduate school orient Lisa?

F

Situation 1

1. B   2. A   3. C   4. B   5. B

Situation 2

1. B   2. A   3. C   4. B   5. A

Situation 3

1. C   2. A   3. A   4. C   5. B

G

Answer Key
Training Application Letters
訓練申請信函

Situation 1

1. A   2. A   3. B   4. A   5. C

Situation 2

1. A   2. C   3. C   4. A   5. C

Situation 3

1. B   2. A   3. A   4. A   5. C

I

Situation 4

Eager to understand your dynamic work, I would like to arrange for a three-month stay as a visiting medical physicist in your cancer research center for tumor control.

As you can see in the attached resume, my undergraduate and graduate training in radiotechnology and medical imagery heavily stressed close collaboration among researchers. I became adept in applying various radiation detection methods. As my graduate research focused on detecting contamination during clinical practice, I had to familiarize myself with the underlying causes of contamination, the extent of the injury caused to humans and a wide array of preventive methods. These academic and professional experiences increased my confidence in planning radiological treatments and implementing radiation detection and protection strategies during therapeutic treatment.

Your cancer research center has distinguished itself in developing novel radiotherapy methods that have greatly benefited patients, as evidenced by your frequent publications in international journals. Your center is widely admired for its strict adherence to quality standards in tumor therapy, as well as its frequent journal publications on novel radiotherapeutic procedures and clinical findings. If successful in securing this visiting researcher position, I will bring my professional knowledge in such areas as detecting radiation dose in the workplace, planning appropriate radiotherapy and devising appropriate shielding for a radiotherapy room.

Regarding my specific interests during this research stay, I am especially interested in the importance of dose detection to radiation security. This interest demands not only becoming proficient in the use of many radiation detection methods, but also understanding the applicability of such methods in a clinical hospital setting. I believe that I possess the necessary practical and theoretical skills as a medical physiologist to contribute to a patient's well-being and simultaneously maintain radiation security. I believe that your organization would be an excellent starting point for me to begin on this career path. I look forward to your thoughts regarding this proposed stay.

Yours truly,

Melody Wu

Situation 5

The opportunity to serve in a self-supported guest researcher position in your radiation dosimetry laboratory would help me become more proficient in this line of research. As a highly adept investigator in the laboratory, I have learned not only how to comprehend fully how seemingly opposite fields are related to each other, but also to handle complex projects that forced me to apply theoretical concepts in a practical context. Such practical work experience has greatly enhanced my competence in accumulating pertinent data and analyzing problems independently.

Having received a Bachelor's degree in Atomic Science and a Master's degree in Medical Imagery, I am well aware of the theoretical and practical issues around radiation. As reflected by the attached resume, my undergraduate studies in atomic physics led me thoroughly to understand how radiation affects materials. Additionally, my active participation in radiation dosimetry-related projects taught me how to measure an actual dose from any radiation source, including photons, electrons, neutrons, X-rays and gamma rays. Hopefully, you will find these skills to be invaluable to any research collaboration in which I am involved at your laboratory.

As a leader in radiation dosimetry research, your laboratory would provide an excellent environment for me to build on my above academic experiences so that I can expand my research activities and grasp many helpful concepts related to the latest technological trends. The impressive training courses that your laboratory offers reflect your excellence in leadership and commitment to staff excellence.

As for the details of this proposed researcher position, I am intrigued with the increasing importance of radiotherapy, especially given the rising cancer death rate. Radiotherapy is especially attractive since it does not involve injecting the patient, yet yields curative effects rapidly. Hopefully, by working directly under your supervision, I will gain further exposure to the latest techniques in this field. Please do not hesitate to contact me for an interview if this proposal is feasible.

Yours truly,

Matt Hsiao

Situation 6

I would like to arrange for a stay as a self-supported guest worker in your biotechnology company for six months. The fundamental and advanced research capabilities I acquired in graduate school have not only nurtured my talent in approaching biotechnology through a multidisciplinary approach, but also widened my range of interests and helped me to grasp fully the latest concepts in biotechnology.

Having immersed myself in the field of radiation for quite some time, I recently completed a Master's degree in Life Sciences at National Cheng Kung University, with a particular interest in researching biology-related topics. While pursuing this Master's degree, I conducted biotechnology-related research at the Animal Technology Institute of Taiwan. As shown in the attached resume, graduate level research prepared me for the rigorous demands of experimentation and, then, the publishing of experimental findings in domestic and international journals. Overall, my participation in research projects that encompassed seemingly unrelated fields reflects my willingness to absorb tremendous amounts of information and manage my time efficiently, an attribute which I believe that your company looks for in its research staff.

As a leader in the biotechnology field, your company has been able to combine commercial success with innovation. Your company has also distinguished itself in the healthcare sector. I am especially impressed with your company's creativity in using standard operating procedures to create state-of-the-art product technologies. Participating in the innovative research projects at your company would further strengthen my expertise in biotechnology and, hopefully, contribute to your ongoing efforts.

I am increasingly drawn to biotechnology, an emerging global field in the new century. Its emergence reflects an increasing emphasis on health, which accompanies an increase in the elderly population worldwide. To become proficient in this area, I must acquire further laboratory experience, explaining why I am seeking a valuable training opportunity at your company. The opportunity to work in a practicum internship in your company would provide me with an excellent environment not only to realize my career aspirations fully, but also to improve my own technological expertise. Please contact me if such an opportunity arises.

Yours truly,

John Wang

J

1. Why did Melody herself with the underlying causes of contamination?

   because her graduate research focused on detecting it during clinical practice

2. Why is the cancer research center widely admired?

   owing to its strict adherence to quality standards in tumor therapy, as well as its frequent journal publications on novel radiotherapeutic procedures and clinical findings

3. Why is Melody confident in her ability to contribute to a patient's well-being and simultaneously maintain radiation security?

   because she possesses the necessary practical and theoretical skills as a medical physiologist

K

1. In what areas has practical work experience greatly enhanced Matt's competence?

   in accumulating pertinent data and analyzing problems independently

2. What did Matt's active participation in radiation dosimetry-related projects teach him?

   how to measure an actual dose from any radiation source, including photons, electrons, neutrons, X-rays and gamma rays

3. What is especially attractive to Matt about radiotherapy?

It does not involve injecting the patient, yet yields curative effects rapidly

L

1. How is John's willingness to absorb tremendous amounts of information and manage time efficiently demonstrated?

by his participation in research projects that encompassed seemingly unrelated fields

2. How has the company that John is applying to distinguished itself in the healthcare sector?

by its creativity in using standard operating procedures to create state-of-the-art product technologies

3. How would participating in the innovative research projects at the company benefit John?

They would further strengthen his expertise in biotechnology.

M

1. What increased Melody's confidence in planning radiological treatments and implementing radiation detection and protection strategies during therapeutic treatment?

2. How did Matt become well aware of the theoretical and practical issues around radiation?

3. What reflects an increasing emphasis on health?

N

Situation 4

1. C   2. A   3. C   4. B   5. A

Situation 5

Answer Key
Training Application Letters
訓練申請信函

1. C   2. A   3. B   4. A   5. C

Situation 6

1. B   2. B   3. C   4. B   5. A

O

Situation 4

1. B   2. C   3. A   4. C   5. B

Situation 5

1. A   2. B   3. B   4. C   5. B

Situation 6

1. B   2. C   3. A   4. C   5. B

Answer Key
Employment Recommendation Letters
就業推薦信函

A

Situation 1

Recommending Mary Li for employment in your globally renowned corporation is indeed an honor. Over the past two years that I have supervised her in the product development group, I have been most impressed by Mary's energy, as evidenced by her seemingly endless perseverance in handling tedious and detailed tasks. Also, her proactive approach towards learning has undoubtedly enabled her to improve her knowledge skills continuously. Given your company's commitment to excellence in product technology and customer service, I cannot think of a better qualified employee.

Mary is a highly motivated individual. In our product development group, she was responsible for performing various experimental procedures and analyzing the results. Her diligence in collecting and organizing materials within the laboratory played an important role in our product development efforts. She has the unique ability to identify exactly what is required for a particular research objective. She also quickly understands the limitations of conventional research. Moreover, she undertook numerous experiments, attempting to solve problems from various angles. Remaining confident despite occasional setbacks, she persevered during experimental work, ultimately yielding commercial success.

She is extremely well prepared for any assigned task. In our product development efforts, she constantly reviewed the latest technological developments and discussed her observations in detail with colleagues. During our weekly group meetings, which often involved discussion of journals and case reports, she actively participated, offering carefully composed questions and responses to other group members. Furthermore, her analytical skills are exemplary. Although occasionally unfamiliar with a particular technology development at the outset, she would analyze the most pertinent information and then quickly identify the project goals and anticipated results.

I have no qualms in recommending this highly motivated individual for employment in your organization. Her creativity and cooperative nature will be a great asset to any future product development effort in which she is involved. Your corporation's great working environment, combined with the impressive number and diversity of training courses to maintain the competence of its employees in the market place, would definitely ensure the ongoing development of Mary's professional skills while helping to improve the living standard of your customers. Feel free to contact me if I can provide you with further information.

Yours truly,

John Wang

Situation 2

The opportunity for Jerry Su to gain professional competence in an eminent organization such as yours is a marvelous one. As his academic advisor who supervised his doctoral level research and dissertation, I feel that I am in a good position to assess this highly competent individual. Jerry's unique ability to integrate and explain seemingly contradictory concepts to those outside of his field of expertise is invaluable in the workplace as it can help provide enough details to managers to enable them to make management decisions based on that information. As a leader, he applied his excellent communication skills to identify fellow classmates' needs and incorporate their opinions in forming laboratory policies.

As a student, he worked diligently to develop his natural talents and displayed seemingly endless energy while under my instruction. I was particularly struck by his total commitment to the task at hand. His intelligence, industry and dedication will undoubtedly support his future employment. Armed with a passion for science, Mr. Li actively participated in several National Science Council-sponsored research projects. His maturity and diligence helped him to focus, as evidenced by his strong analytical skills and sound ability to formulate opinions after synthesizing available knowledge. Undoubtedly, these capabilities significantly contributed to his academic achievements, but will also ensure his future success.

His diligent attitude to studying never ceased to amaze me. For instance, whenever encountering a research bottleneck, he consistently delved into reading and investigating the source of the problem while consulting with me on how to solve it. Since graduation, he has continued to maintain contact with several researchers in the field, discussing issues relating to their clinical or research experience. In addition, his critical thinking skills are remarkable, as evidenced by his ability to synthesize pertinent reading, identify limitations of previous literature and then state the logical next step from a unique perspective.

I do not hesitate in most highly recommending Jerry for employment in your organization. Do not hesitate to contact me if I can provide you with any further insight into this highly qualified individual.

Yours sincerely,

Professor Lisa Lu

Situation 3
I have encouraged Matt Chen to seek employment with your company for quite some time. As his graduate school advisor, I can not think of a more qualified individual for implement your organization's innovative technology developments.

Matt is methodical and thorough in the task set before him, regardless of whether it is academic or professional. Graduate study equipped him with the required knowledge skills and fundamental professional expertise in industrial management. The graduate curriculum markedly differed from his undergraduate curriculum, offering many opportunities for him to strengthen his research fundamentals. For instance, the theoretical and practical concepts taught in the graduate curriculum increased his ability to solve problems logically and straightforwardly. Additionally, the theoretical knowledge and practical laboratory experience gained at graduate school were equally important in allowing him to foster his fundamental research skills. Given his deep interest in quality control, he is committed to pursuing a career in industrial management. In sum, graduate school equipped him with much knowledge and logical competence to address problems in the workplace effectively - attributes that you will find attractive to your company.

I am also impressed with Matt's intuition when adapting to new environments. At graduate school, while learning how to adopt different perspectives in approaching a particular problem during undergraduate training, he acquired several statistical and analytical skills. Doing so involved learning how to analyze problems, identify potential solutions, and implement those solutions according to concepts taught in the classroom. The graduate school curricula equipped him not only with the academic fundamentals required for a management-related career, but also with the workplace skills to meet the rigorous challenges of the intensely competitive hi-tech sector. Securing employment in your company would definitely allow him to realize fully his career aspirations.

I am quite confident of Matt's ability to contribute significantly to any collaborative effort in which he is involved in your company. Please contact me if I can be of further assistance.

Answer Key
Employment Recommendation Letters
就業推薦信函

Yours truly,

Professor Jason Ling

B

1. What played an important role in the product development effort?

   Mary's diligence in collecting and organizing materials within the laboratory

2. What ultimately yielded commercial success?

   Mary's experimental work

3. What did Mary do when actively participated during weekly group meetings?

   She offered carefully composed questions and responses to other group members.

C

1. Why was Jerry able to identify fellow classmates' needs and incorporate their opinions in forming laboratory policies?

   because he applied his excellent communication skills

2. Why was Jerry able to focus during his active participation in several National Science Council-sponsored research projects?

   because of his maturity and diligence

3. Why are Jerry's critical thinking skills remarkable?

   owing to his ability to synthesize pertinent reading, identify limitations of previous literature and then state the logical next step from a unique perspective

D

1. How did Matt's graduate curriculum markedly differ from his undergraduate curriculum?

   It offered many opportunities for him to strengthen his research fundamentals.

2. How did the theoretical and practical concepts taught in the graduate curriculum enable Matt to solve problems? logically and straightforwardly

3. How was Matt able to foster his fundamental research skills?
owing to the theoretical knowledge and practical laboratory experience gained at graduate school

E

1. How frequently were group meetings held?

2. For how long has Jerry continued to maintain contact with several researchers in the field?

3. What is Matt committed to pursuing?

F

Situation 1

1. B   2. C   3. A   4. C   5. B

Situation 2

1. A   2. C   3. B   4. A   5. C

Situation 3

1. B   2. C   3. B   4. B   5. C

G

Situation 1

1. A   2. C   3. A   4. B   5. B

Situation 2

1. B   2. C   3. B   4. B   5. C

Situation 3

1. B   2. B   3. C   4. A   5. B

Answer Key
Employment Recommendation Letters
就業推薦信函

I

Situation 4

I was pleased to hear that Susan Chuang is seeking employment in your company. Susan is widely respected throughout our company, as I have heard often, as her group leader. While collaborating with her in various activities, I became aware of her exemplary communication and leadership skills. Her passion and resolve to pursue a management career also impressed me. Additionally, her refined coordinating skills and direct communication style have facilitated the smooth implementation of several events and company policies. Her strong leadership potential will definitely prove to be a valuable asset to your company.

Susan is truly an adaptable individual. For instance, her familiarity with the implementation different strategies for various purposes allowed her to transfer to a new position in which she was responsible for simplifying administrative procedures and effectively managing personnel. Consequently, group morale was significantly raised owing to increased departmental efficiency. By constantly pursuing her research interests, she actively remained abreast of the latest technological developments and strived diligently to grasp their practical implementations. As your company has distinguished itself in providing high-quality technology products and services, I believe that you will find that Susan's professional experience and knowledge skills can easily blend into your product development team's innovative efforts. As a member of your organization's highly qualified staff, she would offer much research expertise in her area of specialization.

Susan's strong desire to improve her research capabilities constantly is reflected in her active participation in a collaborative project for our company, in which she analyzed customer data and then accumulated it in a novel database for statistical software purposes. Carefully analyzing the data revealed unique facts about the company's particular circumstances, which provided valuable references for administrators who had to make marketing-related decisions. In a similar development, Susan spearheaded our department's development of a novel administrative procedure for classifying and simplifying customers' financial information, processed by our company's accounting division. A database containing detailed customer information is accessed while ensuring the confidentiality of such information, thus reducing administrative costs and the number of personnel involved.

I, therefore, have no hesitation in strongly recommending this individual to your corporate family. Your Human Resources Department is welcome to contact me for further insight into this highly qualified candidate.

Yours truly,

Mary Kuan

Situation 5

I am pleased to recommend John Chang for employment in your organization. Mr. Chang has been an associate researcher at our laboratory for five years. During this period, he has been under my supervision.

John is a resourceful individual. While serving as a research assistant when first entering our laboratory, he quickly learned how to coordinate different aspects of a research project, such as filling out weekly progress reports, managing financial affairs, or organizing regularly held seminars and report contents. In addition to providing him with several opportunities to corroborate what he had learned from textbooks in the classroom, participation in several of our laboratory's research projects allowed him to extend his knowledge skills to fields outside his academic studies to provide innovative solutions. Moreover, his research often involved deriving complex models and modifying laboratory practices to meet a specific research requirement. He also attended several international conferences, which further widened his professional exposure. Moreover, intensive laboratory training definitely enhanced his ability to respond effectively to unforeseen bottlenecks in research.

In addition to his rich academic training and sound knowledge skills, John has many strong personality traits, as evidenced by his positive attitude towards challenges as he continuously strives for higher standards. He brings to your company a decade of experience in the chemical industry. After receiving a Bachelor's degree in Chemistry from National Chung Hsing University in 1993, he secured employment as a chemical engineer at Johnson Chemical Company. In this capacity, he acquired advanced knowledge skills by actively participating in many process development-related projects. He later joined Dupree Chemical Company in 1996, where he served as senior engineer responsible for process control. I believe that you will find such experience to be valuable to your highly qualified staff.

I fully endorse John in his desire to work in your company. Please contact me if I can provide any further insight into Mr. Chang's ability.

Yours truly,
Jerry Su

Situation 6
Given her ability to grasp abstract concepts quickly and her willingness to accept others' constructive criticism to be more effective in an assigned task, I highly recommend Kelly Lin for employment in your organization. Responsible for evaluating her work performance evaluations at our company over the past

four years, I am in a unique position to assess her character and willingness to collaborate closely with other colleagues. She has the unique characteristic of examining a diverse array of topics and, then, searching for their possible relationship in the workplace to increase productivity. Moreover, she also easily adjusts to various organizational positions, reaffirming my conviction that flexibility is essential to strong interpersonal relations. As your company is renowned for its strong organizational culture and management structure, I firmly believe that employing such an innovative individual would be of greatly benefit.

Kelly's strong commitment to the marketing profession is demonstrated by a project that she spearheaded to identify effective demographic variables and forecast accurately growth trends of our company's products and services. Given its effectiveness and accuracy, financial planners have already used this model in estimating consumer demand in the hi-tech sector. Kelly also initiated a similar project aimed at developing an efficient product control system capable of monitoring the manufacturing capacity of our factory production line. The system subsequently developed by her team not only evaluates precisely bottlenecks in production, but also determines immediately the current output and efficiency of the production line. Her success in these projects reflects her adeptness in generating beneficial results that will contribute to corporate revenues, an attribute which I believe that your company is seeking.

I am highly confident of Kelly's ability to meet the rigorous work demands of your research team. As your company offers a competitive work environment for highly skilled professionals, I believe that she will be a welcome addition to your corporate family. Feel free to contact me if I can provide you with further information.

Yours truly,
Julianne Wang

J

1. Why was Susan able to transfer to a new position in which she was responsible for simplifying administrative procedures and effectively managing personnel?

   because of her familiarity with the implementation different strategies for various purposes

2. Why was Susan able to actively remain abreast of the latest technological developments and strive diligently to grasp their practical implementations?

   because she constantly pursued her research interests

3. Why was Susan able to understand unique facts about the company's particular circumstances, which provided valuable references for administrators who had to make marketing-related decisions?

   because she carefully analyzed the data

K

1. How did John extend his knowledge skills to fields outside his academic studies?

   by participating in several of the laboratory's research projects

2. How did John often meet a specific research requirement?

   by deriving complex models and modifying laboratory practices

3. How did John enhance his ability to respond effectively to unforeseen bottlenecks in research?

   through intensive laboratory training

L

1. What reaffirms Julianne's conviction that flexibility is essential to strong interpersonal relations?

   the fact that Kelly easily adjusts to various organizational positions

2. What demonstrates Kelly's strong commitment to the marketing profession?

a project that she spearheaded to identify effective demographic variables and forecast accurately growth trends of our company's products and services

3. What is an attribute of Kelly's that Julianne believes that the company is seeking?

adeptness in generating beneficial results that will contribute to corporate revenues

M

1. What can easily blend into the product development team's innovative efforts?
2. When did Jerry serve as a research assistant?
3. What is the product control system developed in Julianne's project capable of doing?

N

Situation 4
1. B   2. A   3. B   4. C   5. A

Situation 5
1. B   2. B   3. A   4. C   5. B

Situation 6
1. A   2. C   3. B   4. B   5. B

O

Situation 4
1. B   2. C   3. B   4. A   5. C

Situation 5
1. A   2. C   3. A   4. C   5. B

Situation 6
1. A   2. C   3. B   4. C   5. B

About the Author

Born on his father's birthday, Ted Knoy received a Bachelor of Arts in History at Franklin College of Indiana (Franklin, Indiana) and a Master's degree in Public Administration at American International College (Springfield, Massachusetts). He is currently a Ph.D. student in Education at the University of East Anglia (Norwich, England). Having conducted research and independent study in New Zealand, Ukraine, Scotland, South Africa, India, Nicaragua and Switzerland, he has lived in Taiwan since 1989 where he has been a permanent resident since 2000.

Having taught technical writing in the graduate school programs of National Chiao Tung University (Institute of Information Management, Institute of Communications Engineering, Institute of Technology Management, Department of Industrial Management, Department of Transportation Management and, currently, in the College of Management) and National Tsing Hua University (Computer Science, Life Science, Electrical Engineering, Power Mechanical Engineering, Chemistry and Chemical Engineering Departments) since 1989, Ted also teaches in the Institute of Business Management at Yuan Pei University of Science and Technology. He is also the English editor of several technical and medical journals and publications in Taiwan.

Ted is author of The Chinese Technical Writers' Series, which includes <u>An English Style Approach for Chinese Technical Writers</u>, <u>English Oral Presentations for Chinese Technical Writers</u>, <u>A Correspondence Manual for Chinese Technical Writers</u>, <u>An Editing Workbook for Chinese Technical Writers</u> and <u>Advanced Copyediting Practice for Chinese Technical Writers</u>. He is also author of The

Chinese Professional Writers' Series, which includes <u>Writing Effective Study Plans</u>, <u>Writing Effective Work Proposals</u>, <u>Writing Effective Employment Application Statements</u>, <u>Writing Effective Career Statements</u>, <u>Effectively Communicating Online</u>, <u>Writing Effective Marketing Promotional Materials</u>, <u>Effective Management Communication and Effective Business Communication</u>.

Ted created and coordinates the Chinese On-line Writing Lab (OWL) at www. cc.nctu.edu.tw/~tedknoy and www.chineseowl.idv.tw

Acknowledgments

Thanks to the following individuals for contributing to this book:

【特別感謝以下人員的貢獻】

國立交通大學工業管理學系　唐麗英教授
魏　源　林姍慧　金新恩　王有志　林麗甄　裴善康　張志偉
蔡志偉

元培科學技術學院 經營管理研究所
許碧芳（所長）　王貞穎　李仁智　陳彥谷　胡惠真　陳碧俞
王連慶　蔡玟純　高青莉　賴姝惠
李雅玎　戴碧美　楊明雄　陳皇助　林宏隆　鍾玠融　李昭蓉
許美菁　葉伯彥　林羿君　吳政龍　鄭凱元　黃志斌　郭美萱
李尉誠　陳靜怡　盧筱嵐　鄭彥均　劉偉翔　彭廣興　林宗瑋
巫怡樺　朱建華

元培科學技術學院 影像醫學研究所
王愛義（所長）　周美榮　顏映君　林孟聰　張雅玲　彭薇莉
張明偉　李玉綸　聶伊辛　黃勝賢
張格瑜　龔慧敏　林永健　呂忠祐　李仁忠　王國偉　李政翰
黃國明　蔡明輝　杜俊元　丁健益　方詩涵　余宗銘　劉力瑛
郭明杰

元培科學技術學院 生物技術研究所
陳媛孃（所長）　范齡文　彭姵華　鄭啓軒　許凱文　李昇憲
陳雪君　鄭凱暹　尤鼎元　陳玉梅　鄭美玲　郭軒中
朱芳儀　周佩穎　吳佳真

國立交通大學管理學院

國立台灣大學　土木工程研究所 陳俊仲

My technical writing students in the Department of Computer Science and Institute of Life Science at National Tsing Hua University, as well as the College of Management at National Chiao Tung University are also appreciated. Thanks to Wang Chen-Yin for her illustrations. Thanks also to Seamus Harris and Bill Hodgson for reviewing this handbook.

有效撰寫英文讀書計畫
Writing Effective Study Plans

作者：柯泰德（**Ted Knoy**）

內容簡介

本書指導準備出國進修的學生撰寫精簡切要的英文讀書計畫，內容包括：表達學習的領域及興趣、展現所具備之專業領域知識、敘述學歷背景及成就等。本書的每個單元皆提供視覺化的具體情境及相關寫作訓練，讓讀者進行實際的訊息運用練習。此外，書中的編修訓練並可加強「精確寫作」及「明白寫作」的技巧。本書適用於個人自修以及團體授課，能確實引導讀者寫出精簡而有效的英文讀書計畫。

本手冊同時為國立清華大學資訊工程學系非同步遠距教學科技英文寫作課程指導範本。

于樹偉／工業技術研究院主任

　　《有效撰寫讀書計畫》一書主旨在提供國人精深學習前的準備，包括：讀書計畫及推薦信函的建構、完成。藉由本書中視覺化訊息的互 及練習，國人可以更明確的掌握全篇的意涵，及更完整的表達心中的意念。這也是本書異於坊間同類書籍只著重在片斷記憶，不求理解最大之處。

王　玫／工業研究技術院、化學工業研究所組長

　　《有效撰寫讀書計畫》主要是針對想要進階學習的讀者，由基本的自我學習經驗描述延伸至未來目標的設定，更進一步強調推薦信函的撰寫，藉由圖片式訊息互 ，讓讀者主 聯想及運用寫作知識及技巧，避免一味的記憶零星的範例；如此一來，讀者可以更清楚表明個別的特質及快速掌握重點。

※若有任何英文文件修改問題，請直接與柯泰德先生聯絡： （03）5724895

特　　價　新台幣**450**元
劃　　撥　**19419482** 清蔚科技股份有限公司
線上訂　四方書網 www.4Book.com.tw
發 行 所　清蔚科技股份有限公司

有效撰寫英文工作提案
Writing Effective Work Proposals

作者：柯泰德（**Ted Knoy**）

內容簡介

許多國人都是在工作方案完成時才開始撰寫相關英文提案，他們視撰寫提案為行政工作的一環，只是消極記錄已完成的事項，而不是積極的規劃掌控未來及現在正進行的工作。如果國人可以在撰寫英文提案時，事先仔細明辨工作計畫提案的背景及目標，不僅可以確保寫作進度、寫作結構的完整，更可兼顧提案相關讀者的興趣強調。本書中詳細的步驟可指導工作提案寫作者達成此一目標。書中的每個單元呈現三個視覺化的情境，提供國人英文工作提案寫作實質訊息，而相關附加的寫作練習讓讀者做實際的訊息運用。此外，本書也非常適合在課堂上使用，教師可以先描述單元情境而讓學生藉由書中練習循序完成具有良好架構的工作提案。書中內容包括：1.工作提案計畫（第一部分）：背景2.工作提案計畫（第二部分）：行動 3.問題描述 4.假設描述 5.摘要撰寫（第一部分）：簡介背景、目標及方法 6.摘要撰寫（第二部分）：歸納希望的結果及其對特定領域的貢獻 7.綜合上述寫成精確工作提案。

唐傳義／國立清華大學資訊工程學系主任

　　本書重點放在如何在工作計畫一開始時便可以用英文來規劃整個工作提案，由工作提案的背景、行 、方法及預期的結果漸次教導國人如何寫出具有良好結構的英文工作提案。如此用英文明確界定工作提案的程序及工作目標更可以確保英文工作提案及工作計畫的即時完成。對工作效率而言也有助益。

　　在國人積極加入WTO之後的調整期，優良的英文工作提案寫作能力絕對是一項競爭力快速加分的工具。

※若有任何英文文件修改問題，請直接與柯泰德先生聯絡：（**03**）**5724895**

特　　價　新台幣**450**元
劃　　撥　**19735365** 葉忠賢
線上訂購　**www.ycrc.com.tw**
發 行 所　揚智文化事業股份有限公司

有效撰寫求職英文自傳
Writing Effective Employment Application Statements

作者：柯泰德（**Ted Knoy**）

內容簡介

本書主要教導讀者如何建構良好的求職英文自傳。書中內容包括：1.表達工作相關興趣；2.興趣相關產業描寫；3.描述所參與方案裡專業興趣的表現；4.描述學歷背景及已獲成就；5.介紹研究及工作經驗；6.描述與求職相關的課外活；7.綜合上述寫成精確求職英文自傳。

有效的求職英文自傳不僅必須能讓求職者在企業主限定的字數內精確的描述自身的背景資訊及先前成就，更關鍵 的因素是有效的求職英文自傳更能讓企業主快速明瞭求職者如何應用相關知識技能或其特殊領導特質來貢獻企業主。

書中的每個單元呈現三個視覺化的情境，提供國人求職英文自傳寫作實質訊息，而相關附加的寫作練習讓讀者做實際的訊息運用。此外，本書也非常適合在課堂上使用，教師可以先描述單元情境而讓學生藉由書中練習循序完成具有良好架構的求職英文自傳。

黎漢林／國立交通大學管理學院院長

我國加入WTO後，國際化的腳步日益加快；而企業人員之英文寫作能力更形重要。它不僅可促進國際合作夥伴間的溝通，同時也增加了國際客戶的信任。因此國際企業在求才時無不特別注意其員工的英文表達能力。

柯泰德先生著作《有效撰寫求職英文自傳》即希望幫助求職者能以英文有系統的介紹其能力、經驗與抱負。這本書是柯先生有關英文寫作的第八本專書，柯先生教學與編書十分專注，我相信這本書對求職者是甚佳的參考書籍。

※若有任何英文文件修改問題，請直接與柯泰德先生聯絡：（03）5724895

特　　價　新台幣450元
劃　　撥　**19419482** 清蔚科技股份有限公司
線上訂　四方書網 **www.4Book.com.tw**
發 行 所　清蔚科技股份有限公司

有效撰寫英文職涯經歷
Writing Effective Career Statements

作者：柯泰德（**Ted Knoy**）

內容簡介

本書主要教導讀者如何建構良好的英文職涯經歷。書中內容包括：1.表達工作相關興趣；2.興趣相關產業描寫；3.描述所參與方案裡專業興趣的表現；4.描述學歷背景及已獲成就；5.介紹研究及工作經驗；6.描述與求職相關的課外活；7.綜合上述寫成英文職涯經歷。

有效的職涯經歷描述不僅能讓再度就業者在企業主限定的字數內精準的描述自身的背景資訊及先前工作經驗及成就，更關鍵 的，有效的職涯經歷能讓企業主快速明瞭求職者如何應用相關知識技能及先前的就業經驗結合來貢獻企業主。

書中的每個單元呈現六個視覺化的情境，經由以全民英語檢定為標準而設計的口說訓練、聽力、閱讀及寫作四種不同功能來強化英文能力。此外，本書也非常適合在課堂上使用，教師可以先描述單元情境而讓學生藉由書中練習循序在短期內完成。

林進財／元培科學技術學院校長

　　　　近年來，台灣無不時時刻刻地努力提高國際競爭力，不論政府或企業界求才皆以英文表達能力為主要考量之一。唯有員工具備優秀的英文能力，才足以把本身的能力、工作經驗與國際競爭舞台接軌。

　　　　柯泰德先生著作《有效撰寫英文職涯經歷》，即希望幫助已有工作經驗的求職者能以英文有效地介紹其能力、工作經驗與成就。此書是柯先生有關英文寫作的第九本專書，相信對再度求職者是進入職場絕佳的工具書。

※若有任何英文文件修改問題，請直接與柯泰德先生聯絡：（03）5724895

特　　　價　新台幣**480**元
劃　　　撥　**19735365** 葉忠賢
線上訂購　**www.ycrc.com.tw**
發 行 所　揚智文化事業股份有限公司

有效撰寫專業英文電子郵件
Effectively Communicating Online

作者：柯泰德（**Ted Knoy**）

內容簡介

本書主要教導讀者如何建構良好的專業英文電子郵件。書中內容包括：1.科技訓練請求信函；2.資訊交流信函；3.科技訪問信函；4.演講者邀請信函；5.旅行安排信函；6.資訊請求信函。

書中的每個單元呈現三個視覺化的情境，經由以全民英語檢定為標準而設計的口說訓練、聽力、閱讀及寫作四種不同功能來強化英文能力。此外，本書也非常適合在課堂上使用，教師可以先描述單元情境而讓學生藉由書中練習循序在短期內完成。

許碧芳／元培科學技術學院經營管理研究所所長

隨著時代快速變遷，人們生活步調及習性也十倍速的演變。舉郵件為例，由早期傳統的郵局寄送方式改為現今的電子郵件（e-mail）系統。速度不但但快且也節省費用。對有時效性的訊息傳送更可達事半功倍的效果。不僅如此，電子郵件不受地域的限制，可以隨地進行溝通，也是生活及職場上一項利器。

柯先生所著《有效撰寫專業英文電子郵件》，乃針對目前對電子郵件寫作需求，配合六種不同情境展示近兩百個範例寫作。藉此觀摩他人電子郵件寫作來加強讀者本身的寫作技巧，同時配合書中網路練習訓練英文聽力及閱讀技巧。是一本非常實且符合網路時代需求的工具書。

※若有任何英文文件修改問題，請直接與柯泰德先生聯絡：（**03**）**5724895**

特價　新台幣**520**元
劃撥 **19735365** 葉忠賢
線上訂購 **www.ycrc.com.tw**
發行所　揚智文化事業股份有限公司

有效撰寫行銷英文
Writing Effective Marketing Promotional Materials

作者：柯泰德（**Ted Knoy**）

內容簡介

本書主要教導讀者如何建構良好的行銷英文。書中內容包括：1.預測市場趨勢；2.產品或服務研發；3.專案描述；4.公司或組織介紹；5.組或部門介紹；6.科技介紹；7.工業介紹。

書中的每個單元呈現六個視覺化的情境，經由以全民英語檢定為標準而設計的口說訓練、聽力、閱讀及寫作四種不同功能來強化英文能力。此外，本書也非常適合在課堂上使用，教師可以先描述單元情境而讓學生藉由書中練習循序在短期內完成。

李鍾熙 / 工業科技研究院院長

　　本書特別針對行銷英文加以解說並輔以範例，加深讀者之印象，並以六個視覺化的情境，訓練讀者的口說、聽力、閱讀及寫作能力，是從事國際行銷、管理工作者值得參閱的書籍。

※若有任何英文文件修改問題，請直接與柯泰德先生聯絡：（**03**）**5724895**

　　　　　　特價　新台幣**450**元
　　　　　　劃撥 **19735365** 葉忠賢
　　　　　　線上訂購 **www.ycrc.com.tw**
　　　　　　發行所　揚智文化事業股份有限公司

管理英文
Effective Management Communication

作者：柯泰德（**Ted Knoy**）

內容簡介

本書為「應用英文寫作系列」之第七本書，主要訓練管理人才（管理師）撰寫符合工作場合需要的書面英文。書中內容包括：1.有效撰寫管理英文備忘錄─調查性 與建議性報告；2.有效撰寫管理英文備忘錄─說服力的展現；3.有效撰寫管理英文備忘錄─非正式實用管理技術報告；4.有效海外管理英文交流──探討管理 師如何有效的與海外專業人士交流英文；5.管理師專業英文工作經歷撰寫；6.有效撰寫英文工作提案；7.管理師學術及專業訓練英文申請撰寫；8.有效進行 管理英文口語簡報；9.管理英文寫作上之常見問題；10.求職申請信函；11.專業訓練申請信函；12.求職推荐信函。

書中列出許多範例與練習，主要是幫助讀者糾正常犯寫作格式上錯誤，由反覆練習中，進而熟能生巧提升有關個人管理方面的英文寫作能力。

※若有任何英文文件修改問題，請直接與柯泰德先生聯絡：（03）5724895

特價　新台幣**450**元
劃撥 **19735365** 葉忠賢
線上訂購 **www.ycrc.com.tw**
發行所　揚智文化事業股份有限公司

商用英文
Effective Business Communication

作者：柯泰德（**Ted Knoy**）

內容簡介

本書為「應用英文寫作系列」之第八本書，書中練習題部分主要是幫助國人糾正常犯寫作錯誤，由反覆練習中，進而熟能生巧提升有關英文商業策略的寫作能力。書 中內容包括：1.統計結果的推論及應用；2.描述組織或科技需求；3.描述產業所面臨的困境；4.方案結果的總結；5.描述公司最新的科技成就；6.產品／服務銷售實例；7.產品／服務開發的未來動向及挑戰。

書中的每個單元呈現三個視覺化的情境，經由以全民英語檢定為標準而設計的口說訓練，聽力，閱讀及寫作四種不同功能來強化英文總體能力。此外，書中附的解答 使得本書也非常適合在課堂上使用，教師可以先描述單元情境而讓學生藉由書中練習循序在短期內完成。不論是小組或個人皆可由書中的練習寫出更精確的英文商業策略。

李鍾熙／工業科技研究院院長

　　本書特別針對行銷英文加以解說並輔以範例，加深讀者之印象，並以六個視覺化的情境，訓練讀者的口說、聽力、閱讀及寫作能力，是從事國際行銷、管理工作者值得參閱的書籍。

※若有任何英文文件修改問題，請直接與柯泰德先生聯絡：（**03**）**5724895**

　　　　　　　　特價　新台幣**480**元
　　　　　　　　劃撥 **19735365** 葉忠賢
　　　　　　　　線上訂購 **www.ycrc.com.tw**
　　　　　　　　發行所　揚智文化事業股份有限公司

The Chinese Online Writing Lab
【柯泰德線上英文論文編修訓練服務】

您有科技英文寫作上的困擾嗎？
您的文章在投稿時常被國外論文審核人員批評文法很爛嗎？以至於被退稿嗎？
您對論文段落的時式使用上常混淆不清嗎？
您在寫作論文時同一個 詞或名詞常常重複使用嗎？

您的這些煩惱現在均可透過柯泰德網路線上科技英文論文編修服務來替您
加以解決。本服務項目分別含括如下：

1. 英文論文編輯與修改
2. 科技英文寫作開課訓練服務
3. 線上寫作家教
4. 免費寫作格式建議服務，及網頁問題討論區解答
5. 線上遠距教學（互 練習）

另外，為能廣為服務中國人士對論文寫作上之 點，柯泰德亦同時著作下列
參考書籍可供有志人士為寫作上之參考。

＜1.精通科技論文（報告）寫作之捷徑
＜2.做好英文會議簡報
＜3.英文信函參考手冊
＜4.科技英文編修訓練手冊
＜5.科技英文編修訓練手冊（進階篇）
＜6.有效撰寫英文讀書計畫

上部分亦可由柯泰德先生的首頁中下載得到。
如果您對本服務有興趣的話，可參考柯泰德先生的首頁標示。

柯泰德網路線上科技英文論文編修服務
地址：新竹市大學路50號8樓之三
TEL:03-5724895
FAX:03-5724938
網址：http://www.cc.nctu.edu.tw/~tedknoy
E-mail:tedaknoy@ms11.hinet.net

應用英文寫作系列 09

科技英文

作　　者／柯泰德（Ted Knoy）
出 版 者／揚智文化事業股份有限公司
發 行 人／葉忠賢
總 編 輯／閻富萍
執行編輯／胡琡珮
地　　址／新北市深坑區北深路三段 260 號 8 樓
電　　話／(02)8662-6826
傳　　真／(02)2664-7633
網　　址／http://www.ycrc.com.tw
　E-mail　／service@ycrc.com.tw
印　　刷／鼎易印刷事業股份有限公司
　ISBN　／978-986-298-011-8
初版一刷／2011 年 7 月
定　　價／新台幣 450 元

國家圖書館出版品預行編目（CIP）資料

科技英文 / 柯泰德 (Ted Knoy). -- 初版. -- 新北
市：揚智文化, 2011.07
面； 公分. -- （應用英文寫作系列；7）
ISBN 978-986-298-011-8（平裝）

1.英語 2.科學技術 3.寫作法

805.17   100012685